H🐽gs Back Books

– a nose for a good book ...

Published by
Hogs Back Books
34 Long Street, Devizes
Wiltshire
SN10 1NT
www.hogsbackbooks.com

First published in Great Britain in 2020 by Hogs Back Books

Printed in Malta by Melita Press
ISBN: 978-1-907432-53-8
British Library Cataloguing-in-Publication Data.
A catalogue record for this book is available
from the British Library.
1 3 5 4 2

INKY STEVENS –
THE CASE OF THE CARETAKER'S KEYS

Chris Martin

Hogs Back Books

For Dad.

Thanks to June for her all her love and support; to Ann, Bob and Andy, Paul and Karen Ross, and Ian Grozdanovic. Also, thanks to John Winstanley for all his guidance. Plus a huge thank you to Karen Stevens at Hogs Back Books for seeing a glimmer of potential in the Great School Detective and being willing to take a chance on him. (Her surname, I'm assured, being one of life's lucky coincidences.)

Facebook: Inky Stevens the Great School Detective.
Website: www.chrismartinwriter.com

PROLOGUE

A week after Blinkton's Great Storm, a tall, dark figure set off to finish what he'd started; his jaw was set, his features a mask of resolve.

It was well past midnight by the time the intruder slipped inside Blinkton High School. As he waited for his eyes to adjust, drops of rainwater slid from his leather coat, spotting the floor beneath, while all around an intense blackness spread out over the Reception area like ink on blotting paper. Everything was still.

Reassured, the intruder set about his business with a confidence rarely seen in someone so young. He stole along the labyrinth of corridors, scarcely troubling the air, his crisp footsteps following him into the darkness.

The figure exited the main building and crossed the rain-swept yard towards a plain-looking office in the old part of the school. He unlocked its door and slipped inside. Immediately, the intruder snapped on his torch, and a funnel of intense, white light sliced through the confined space, causing shadows to pool around his eyes like those of a Halloween mask.

"So far, so good," he muttered to himself.

The intruder continued his task with the precision of a watchmaker. Squinting, he unlocked the thick, iron door to his left. The cavernous space that revealed itself – the school's vault – hadn't changed since his last visit. His expression remained fixed, as he beheld rows of shelves stretching back into the darkness, but he had no time to marvel at the vault's vastness, nor its orderliness; instead he made his way purposefully down the central aisle. Reaching above his head, he swiftly located the relevant file and removed a sheaf of papers. From these, he quickly identified the item he was after: a single brown envelope.

"How is it that such a plain-looking item can carry so much weight?" he thought.

Instinctively, the intruder tore it open and extracted a piece of A4 paper from within. He angled his torch down onto the document. Just as before, his skin prickled at the horror of what he read. He folded the paper in half and in half again, and placed it in his rucksack. He then switched it for an identical looking sheet with a smile so faint that it scarcely troubled his pale face.

The intruder returned the file to its rightful place and retraced his steps to the smaller office, where he snapped off his torch before stepping back out into the yard.

Outside, with the remnants of the Great Storm drumming on the tarmac, he lifted his head heavenwards and breathed in the icy sharpness of the night before turning swiftly and melting away into the night …

CHAPTER ONE –
WELCOME TO BLINKTON

Back then, the education delivered to Britain's youngsters was not necessarily better than it is today, but it was a lot simpler: teachers were expected to teach and pupils were expected to learn; pupils tried to create mayhem in the classroom and teachers tried to stop them.

At that time, Blinkton-on-Sea was a dreary coastal town. (It still is.) Twinned with the French town Mal-de-Mer, it suffered greatly by comparison. While Mal-de-Mer basked in Mediterranean sunshine, Blinkton barely lifted its head off its pillow for a few dismal weeks each summer.

Only one train line ventured into Blinkton (just one road too). Other than that, the small coastal town remained isolated, stubbornly clinging to the shoreline like some unsightly whelk or a piece of jetsam snagged on a rock and left to decompose.

The town's secondary school was built around the ruins of an old monastery, perched high on the clifftops. Its frontage, hidden behind a set of iron railings, was dominated by brick, concrete and stainless steel. As a result, it looked down on the town it served with all the charm of an air-raid warning station – or a prison.

And as a school, if the relevant terminology had been around back then, Blinkton High would have been labelled 'requires improvement'. Although the institution contained some well-mannered, diligent pupils, on balance they were rare. The typical Blinkton student preferred to muddle along doing the minimum to get by.

The school's most talented student was unarguably Inky Stevens. 'Inky' was astute, incisive and disciplined, and his talent – that of solving mysteries – was unique and unchallenged. Not that the Great School Detective glamorised his exploits; not at all. He simply went about his business quietly, committed to serving the school community as best he could.

Inky had arrived in Blinkton midway through the third year. Rumour had it that 'complications' during his upbringing meant that for him to continue living with his mother had been deemed 'inadvisable'. As a result, he had been placed in the care of his mother's sister and her husband as a temporary measure, pending a more permanent review. Perhaps it was this that made him such a private individual. Who knows? Inky gave little away about his past. In fact, he rarely spoke at all.

In appearance, Inky was tall and thin, with a bearing that could be described as 'imposing': his skin was vampire-pale, almost translucent; his face thin and drawn; his hair was black, cut short with a choppy sea of curls; his eyes were simultaneously dead, yet very much alive. Inky Stevens, the sleek, self-confident raven of folklore; distinctive, yet anonymous; striking, yet invisible.

Blinkton's Head Teacher, known to everyone as 'the Snake', had decreed that Blinkton High School's uniform would be black and orange, but Inky was not one to conform; his own version comprised the customary trousers and shirt (without tie), over which he wore a long, black, leather coat, which flared at the bottom like a cape. On his feet, he wore black boots in the winkle-picker style. His black, leather belt was studded, and he carried a buffed leather rucksack, in which he kept all the tools needed for his investigations (and occasionally school books too).

Every morning during break time, Blinkton's Great School Detective took up residence backstage in the school hall in a makeshift office. This, once a store for theatrical props and costumes, was set back beyond the stage curtains, hidden behind all manner of discarded rubbish: chairs and tables, blackboards, a plastic model of the solar system, and a broken hockey goal. And it was there at eleven o'clock each weekday, seated on one of the school's plastic chairs, that Inky would be presented with all manner of assignments, and from these he would deliberate at some length on which ones to accept.

CHAPTER TWO –
THE THEFT

That Monday, the third of the new school year, started off no differently to any other day. Inky picked his way backstage after a dreary double English with 'Chalky' Whittle, and while packs of kids charged around in the fresh September air, he settled himself down and began the process of waiting.

The teenage detective was not alone for long before the stage curtains separated, and a shaft of light momentarily flashed across the blackness. This was followed shortly after by the sound of falling wood.

"Argh! Who left that there? Me bloomin' knee!"

These exclamations and the sound of tumbling debris continued as a figure picked his way through the semi-darkness. If the detective was surprised to see Blinkton's caretaker hobble out of the gloom, he didn't show it; he simply stared ahead with dark-eyed indifference.

Fred Varley was wearing his usual caretaker's uniform: ragged jeans, scuffed work boots, cloth cap and a dark blue work jacket, stained with paint and oil. Having reached his destination, he leant against the wall to massage his knee. In doing so, the silhouette of his misshapen ears became visible in the grey light. Inky could also make out a nose which bent slightly to the left and a beard that was matted and unkempt.

"It's true then," said Fred, "the Great School Detective really does hide away here during morning break." He paused briefly, looking for reassurance, before continuing, "I thought it was just a rumour. Not been back 'ere for a while; it's a mess," he laughed weakly.

"Yes?" said Inky. "How can I help you?"

"Well, I've heard that if anyone has a problem, you are the person to assist them, and I have a problem, quite a serious problem." The old man glanced at the teenage detective, then looked away. "It's me keys – the school keys – I don't 'ave 'em anymore. They've been nicked," he said.

Inky's eyes narrowed.

"It's a big bunch of keys," explained Fred. "I keep 'em on a stainless-steel ring. There are all kinds of keys on it: big keys, small keys, brass keys, rusty keys. There's even one antique key, with fancy fretwork on its handle – it's irreplaceable. In fact, there's so many bloomin' keys on that bunch I've forgotten what some of 'em are for. I carry 'em around on a long chain clipped to me jeans. Right here, see?" He lifted his jacket, gesturing towards his waistband.

Fred waited for a response. When none came, he continued, "Anyway, them keys are vital to the running of this school. Some of 'em don't have duplicates."

"And these keys allow access to where?" asked Inky.

"Every-bloomin'-where!" replied Fred. "If there's a lock in this school, then the key to open it is on that stolen bunch. Every classroom, every storeroom, the school minibus, the staffroom, staff lockers, Miss Peters' office drawer, the Art Block, the bike sheds. Plus," he lowered his voice, "there's a fancy key, which unlocks the Snake's office and her safe. Even the key to Broker's Arch is on it!" His expression darkened, "The door to the spiral staircase is unlocked. Anyone could climb up and scamper out onto the archway. It's bloomin' dangerous!"

Fred shifted from one foot to the other, "I have a meeting with the Snake every Thursday morning at nine. She gets me to open the safe to sort out all the paperwork for the staff rotas. What am I goin' to do then, Master Stevens? I can't look into them cold eyes of 'ers and tell 'er I've lost the keys to the whole bloomin' school. She'll destroy me."

Inky felt a surge of pity.

"The whole school is at risk. Whoever took me keys has the run of the place. I can't even lock up me own room." Fred took a tentative step forwards and removed his hat, twisting it in his hands. "Someone took them keys, and I need 'em back. Please can you help me? You're me only hope."

Inky sat motionless, contemplating. Far off, a bell rang, followed by the sound of feet marching their way towards classrooms. Finally, he spoke, "I'd like a little time to think about what you've said and what I might do about it, if indeed I do anything at all. Can you be inside your Maintenance Room at three? If I can help, I'll be there. If not ..." Inky left his sentence hanging, then made to leave, "If you'll excuse me, I have history with Mr Dukes."

The young detective set off for class, carefully negotiating his way through the backstage clutter before emerging into the brightness beyond. As he crossed the playground he plucked a carved crow, the size of chess piece, from his coat pocket. Deep in thought, he began to turn this over and over between slender fingers.

Fred Varley found himself alone in the semi-darkness. He slid his cap back into place and hoped he'd said enough. He needed Inky's help. Who else could he rely on? His thoughts were interrupted by a sharp burst of static, and at once he removed a two-way radio from his belt.

"Fred, where are you?" enquired Blinkton's Receptionist, Ginny Cartwright. "The Snake's on the warpath!"

Fred held his breath.

"You're needed in the junior boys' toilet urgently. The first-years have stuffed toilet paper into the basins and set the taps running – again. It's like Niagara Falls in there. Get a move on! And bring your mop!"

The radio crackled back to silence.

Fred let out a long sigh. Flooding in the boys' toilets was something he could deal with. The old man clipped his radio back onto his belt and shuffled off in the direction of the stage curtains, hands held out in front like Frankenstein's Monster. As he retraced his steps through the gloom, his right knee collided with the corner of an old locker unit.

"Argh, bloomin' 'eck! Me other knee!" he cried.

CHAPTER THREE –
THE SUSPECTS

By the time three o'clock arrived, Fred Varley found himself waiting inside the Maintenance Room. A fluorescent strip light flickered above, adding to his sense of anxiety, and his eyes passed over the vast assortment of clutter that covered every available work surface: tools, nails, screws, discarded batteries, teacups, a chainsaw, mousetraps (one with mouse skeleton attached), an open packet of biscuits and an unopened one, a thickly coiled rope, and a white, plastic telephone. At the centre of the right-hand wall stood a battered locker, its door clinging onto the metal frame by a single hinge. In the far corners sat two chairs: one an old-fashioned, high-backed, chintz recliner; the other a low-sprung, sagging club chair in green. On both, layers of duct tape attempted to restrain stuffing, which seemed determined to escape.

A door at the far end of the room allowed access to the school's boiler room down a set of concrete steps. The boiler itself was affectionately nicknamed 'Old Betty', and she could be plainly heard, gurgling and spluttering away to herself.

As Fred attempted to pace away his nerves, a clock balanced on a nail above his desk ticked away.

Tick, tock, tick, tock …

Fred sat down. He stood up. He sat down again. He stood up again, shuffling back and forth within the confines of his room. Finally, just as he was about to give up, the door swung open, and a distinctive figure was revealed, silhouetted against the pale September light.

Fred overplayed his greeting, "Master Stevens, so good of you to come! Please take a seat."

Inky did as requested.

"Thank you," said the young detective, taking out a black ink pen and well-thumbed notebook from his rucksack. "If I'm to take on your case, I need to hear everything in as much detail as possible."

Fred was unable to contain himself, "The last time I saw me keys was in the Reflection Room last Friday. You know the Reflection Room? It's that room in the RE Department with the big tent inside it – the 'Armony Tent. There's piles of brightly coloured cushions scattered across the floor in there and lots of lamps."

Inky sat motionless, staring at his client.

"There's music playing in there, too – more like sounds really; calming sounds – panpipes, or water trickling, or fire cracklin' an' such like. The Snake keeps that room as a special place where kids can go to …"

"Reflect?" said Inky, raising an eyebrow.

"Yes, well, I was in there for about an hour. It was Lesson Five – the last lesson of the week. The Snake 'ad asked me to change all the 'lectric sockets. They was old, see. So, there I was in the Reflection Room, on me hands and knees, puttin' in these new sockets – just above the skirtin' board. Now, normally, I'd 'ave me keys fixed onto that loop on me jeans so I can slip 'em into me jacket pocket while I work, but they kept fallin' out. Me pocket's ripped, see, so I unclipped 'em and put 'em on the table next to the record player. It was playin' birdsong."

Inky grimaced.

Fred nodded in agreement. "Bloomin' bird noises. "All manner of twitterin' and squawkin'. Dunno 'bout helping anyone to reflect, it just got on me nerves. But," he went on, "I only unclipped me keys 'cos I thought they'd be safe. I wasn't spectin' anyone else to come in."

"But someone did?"

"Four people did, three of 'em schoolkids and one of 'em

staff. I didn't think anything of it at the time. I was just getting on with the job," Fred explained. "When I'd finished, I went to collect me keys from off the table, but they'd gone; vanished! One of them four had nicked 'em!"

"So," Inky continued, "four suspects in total. I need their names, who came in and in what order, how long they stayed and what happened while they were there."

Fred removed his cap. "First it was that fourth-year, Spud Barton," he said, scratching his head. "You know the lad? A bit of a brute with a shaven head and potato face?"

"Everyone knows Spud."

"Well, last Friday he was intent on causing chaos, shouting at the top of his voice, throwin' cushions about, knocking lamps over, zippin' an' unzippin' the 'Armony Tent."

"What did you do?"

"What could I do? I told him he'd no right being in there, but he just laughed, so I told him I was going to get Mr Bennett, and that's when things turned nasty." Fred looked down at the floor.

"I can't help you unless I know everything," said Inky.

Fred slowly lifted his head, "He squared up to me an' said if I breathed a word to anyone, he'd make me life around school a livin' hell. Then he threw a cushion at me, and after that he waved his fist about as if he were goin' to hit me."

"And did he?"

"No, he just laughed, and walked out, whistlin', bloomin' whistling!" Fred caught Inky's eye, "Look, Master Stevens, you won't tell nobody 'bout this?"

"Everything you've told me will be kept in confidence. That's how I operate. So, who next?" asked Inky.

Fred gave a half-hearted smile, "It was that fourth-year glamour-puss – the lass with the hair. Her who strolls around like she's on a catwalk. Long legs. Blonde. Always trowelled in make-up. Her perfume stinks an' all! Oh," he added, desperate to think of anything that could be of use, "she adds things to her uniform: badges and bracelets and hairbands – all kinds of sparkly nonsense. Miss Peters spends half her time confiscating 'em."

"Candy Sugarcane," said Inky. "She's in my form."

"Candy Sugarcane!" Fred's face lit up. "Come on, Master Stevens, that's not her real name?"

"It's not her original name; she changed it last year. She thought she needed a name that would help her stand out in the fashion industry, where she plans to have a career."

Fred shifted in his chair, "Well, it's certainly memorable."

"What was she doing inside the Reflection Room?" continued Inky.

Fred shrugged, "Dunno. She didn't neither. Not a bloomin'

clue. She thought that Miss Clegg had switched her classroom. 'Last thing on a Friday?' I said, 'That's not likely. The Snake's booked me in here to fix the 'lectrics.' But this Candy lass just stood there with a blank expression and said, 'Aww, is it Friday? I can't remember whether Miss Clegg's my teacher for this lesson or not.' Then, as if all this thinkin' 'ad exhausted her, she drifts inside the 'Armony Tent and lays down, sprawled out like she was sunbathin' or summat."

"What did you do?"

"I rang Miss Cartwright to let her know that some confused, orange-faced girl had just decided to have a nap inside the 'Armony Tent. I wanted to make sure it was reported proper, see, and then I got back on with me sockets. Miss Cartwright said she knew exactly who it was. 'Leave her alone,' she said. 'If it's warm in there, she'll be happy enough.' So, I left her in there and went about me business."

"Weren't you concerned?"

"No, I just assumed she'd fallen asleep. Probably 'ad, too. Birdsong makes people drowsy. But when I looked in the tent five minutes later, it were empty.

"Were your keys missing at that point?"

"Sorry, Master Stevens, I never checked the table till I'd finished the job. I don't know when they disappeared or who took 'em. I only know that it was one of them four."

Inky's eyes sparkled in the gloom. "Just two more suspects. Please continue."

Fred screwed up his face, "The new Science Technician came in next. That twiggy-looking fella – all springy hair and pencil-moustache. I don't trust 'im. How can you work with all them chemicals and still have such a pristine lab-coat?"

"Let's stick to the facts," said Inky. "So, Mr Whitkirk was the third person to enter the Reflection Room?"

Fred flushed under his beard, "Yes," he continued, "he 'ad a clipboard in one hand and a roll of tape in t'other. He said Mr Day 'ad asked him to collect a record that he'd left on the table."

"And was this true?"

"Could 'ave been. There was a few LPs lying about. I wasn't really payin' attention. Anyway, Whitty pranced over to the very table from which me keys was snatched.

"But you didn't see him take them?"

"No," said Fred.

"Did you hear the sound of keys jangling?"

"No, I was too busy workin'."

Inky exhaled, "So, how long was Mr Whitkirk inside the Reflection Room?"

"No time at all," said Fred. "He was in and out before his trousers 'ad time to gather a crease."

"I sense that you feel some hostility towards Mr Whitkirk?"

Fred shifted in his chair, "He's a bit of a know-it-all. Thinks he can do me job better than me."

"And this belief stems from when?"

Fred took a second before replying, "Last July, before the guv'nors' meeting in the library, when he mended the coffee machine for me. He said he was just passin' and saw me 'in a spot of bother', so he thought he'd lend a hand." A flicker of anger flared up in Fred's eyes, "Made me look like a right Charlie, he did. I had the back of the machine off and everythin'. Wires everywhere. Coffee swishing about. And he bloomin' breezes in and fixes it in an instant."

"Instant coffee, eh?"

Fred looked up, puzzled.

"It was a joke."

"Oh, well. Anyway," he continued, "do you know how he fixed it?"

Inky shrugged.

"He bloomin' switched it on, didn't he? It was off at the wall. Could 'ave kicked meself, but Whitty was pleased as punch. He gave a weak little 'huh-huh' of a laugh, but it set everyone off, even the Head Guv'nor, Lord Merridew, joined in. And before long, all that lot in the library was laughing at me."

Fred shuffled onto his feet, "I tell you now, Master Stevens, Wilfred Whitkirk makes me blood boil."

Inky noted Fred's change of complexion, "So it would appear."

"*Cufflinks*, Master Stevens!" he growled. "Under his lab-coat, Whitty wears cufflinks. Braces too! He wears red braces! What a … what a …" he struggled to find an appropriate word, "dandy!"

"Okay," said Inky flatly, "let's focus on the case in hand."

Fred sank back into his chair and fished a handkerchief from his pocket to mop his brow. In the pause that followed, the distinctive hum of Old Betty's thermostat kicking in emerged from the boiler room below.

Inky couldn't help but pity the poor old man slumped in front of him, face buried in a dirty handkerchief, which revealed faded lettering: 'VA' – the first two letters of his surname. "You said there was a fourth person?" he continued.

"Yes," said Fred, "it was the little second-year lad with the wire-framed glasses, shiny satchel and side parting – looks a bit like a ventriloquist's dummy. The only kid in school who wears shorts all year round. His dad's that Head Guv'nor fellah I just mentioned – Merridew – him with the pinstripe suit an' bloomin' bowler hat."

"Ah yes, Crispin," said Inky. "I know him. He's clever and conscientious – very much an *individual*. I'm also aware that this makes him a target for bullying."

"Yeah," Fred puffed out his cheeks, "poor mite was in a bit of a state."

"Go on."

"I was on me final socket when I heard the door creak open. I looked up and there was this Crispin kid, hands bunched into the pockets of them shorts of 'is and tears streamin' down 'is face. 'What's up? Kids picking on you, are they?' I said, 'cos I noticed some food was smeared all down 'is front. 'Yeah,' he replied, 'in Cookery, Bridie McMuffin flicked cake mixture at me. Then Kristy Gee hit me on the head with a wooden spoon.' I could see that poor lad were being bullied and me heart went out to 'im."

Inky looked thoughtful, "Had Miss Pinkerton encouraged Crispin to take some time out?"

Fred twisted his cap as though he was squeezing water out of a sponge, "Dunno, but the kid weren't any bother. He just stayed in the Reflection Room for the last ten minutes of the day while I finished off me job. Very polite, he were. He even tidied up all the cushions that Spud 'ad messed up. Then, as soon as the home-time bell rang, he were off like a shot. He couldn't wait to get home."

"I think he would have been heading to the Common Room for Chess Club," said Inky. "Chess is one of Crispin's passions. He plays every Friday after school with Mr Beeston."

"Bloomin' 'eck, I've never heard of kid *wantin'* to stay behind on a Friday. Who wins?"

Inky tilted his head as if to say, 'who do you think?' and then continued, "What happened once Crispin left the Reflection Room?"

"After that, I went to grab me keys off the table, but they was gone," sighed Fred. "Then me mind started racing: 'How the bloomin' 'eck am I going to lock up now?' I thought to meself, 'This is seriously serious. The school's not secure.'" Fred's voice began to falter, "I began to wonder what the Snake would say if she found out. What she'd do. And that's when I started to panic. I mean, I searched for them keys, 'course I did, but I knew where I'd put 'em, and they wasn't there. He slumped forwards, all the colour having drained from his face, "One of them four has stolen me keys. It could be just some silly prank or …"

"Something serious," suggested Inky.

"Exactly!"

Fred slowly began to rock backwards and forwards, his chair creaking out a disjointed rhythm. Inky felt for Fred, but couldn't bring himself to offer any gesture of sympathy. Instead, he turned his mind to the task ahead and began jotting down a summary of what Fred had recounted. "Time is short," he thought, "but there are only four possible suspects – the four visitors to the Reflection Room last Friday: Spud Barton, Candy Sugarcane, Wilfred Whitkirk and Crispin Merridew. This couldn't be too difficult a case to solve."

Inky closed his notebook. "Fred," he said, "this is nothing more than an unfortunate accident. There was no way you could have foreseen the theft of your keys, and I can see the distress their loss is causing you. I've decided to accept your case. Because of your scheduled meeting with the Snake on Thursday, I have little more than two days to complete my investigation. I can only hope that Blinkton School remains safe until then. Now listen carefully: to have the best chance of success, you must keep me informed of any unusual activity that might relate to the missing keys. You can do this by placing a note addressed to me in the morning register. I register in Room 13 with Mr Dukes. Don't try to contact me in any other way."

"That's terrific!" blurted Fred, "Perry is a friend of mine. He comes down here most break times for a cup of tea and a biscuit. I'll have a word with him."

"Fair enough," Inky conceded, "to have Dukes on board might be an asset." Then he added, "To recap: between two and three o'clock last Friday, you were in the Reflection Room replacing electric sockets when someone stole your keys. These keys, some of which are unique, were all hanging from a large stainless-steel ring."

"Yes."

"And you're certain you had them with you when you entered the Reflection Room?"

"Yes."

"And equally certain that they were missing when you left, just over an hour later?"

"Yes."

"And only four people visited the Reflection Room during this time, and of these visits no two overlapped?"

"Correct again, Master Stevens."

"Right," said Inky, getting up to leave, "if I need to speak to you again, I'll find you. If things go according to plan, we won't need to meet until the case has been solved." He spun around in a tight arc and headed to the door. As he tugged the door open, Fred raised a hand against the sharp autumnal light which flooded in.

"One more thing," said Inky, I want you to ring Miss Cartwright now and ask her to collect the unopened packet of biscuits lying on your worktop. Tell her you over-ordered and wondered if she might like them."

"What if she won't accept?"

"Receptionists never refuse biscuits," said Inky.

Fred watched the young detective disappear into the

September glare, filled with relief.

"An angel in black is on my side," he murmured.

CHAPTER FOUR –
ORGANISING THE TROOPS

Inky Stevens did not have friends in the sense that most people would understand the word. Classmates Ross and Rose Berry came the closest to fulfilling that role, but it was a relationship based more on mutual understanding than friendship: when Inky needed help, they'd be there for him, prepared to accept his distant nature in return for the thrill of the chase.

The appearance of a small, black crow above the lintel of their form room door was investigator's signal to his helpers that he had accepted a new assignment. So that Monday evening, Ross and Rose responded in the manner expected of them. After a quick trip home, they immediately shuffled back into their boots and parkas and, with the slam of their front door, raced off to the other side of town.

Since his arrival at Blinkton, Inky had lived with his Aunt

Alice and Uncle Eric in a semi-detached house on Horrobin Lane, part of a new development to the west of Blinkton. And it was there that the twins headed at full tilt.

Brother and sister shot along the promenade, passing the Funshine Arcade and the Codfather Fish and Chip Restaurant on their way. Next, they turned inland and threaded their way through a warren of streets until they arrived at their destination.

"We're here to see Inky," the twins said slightly breathlessly to the middle-aged woman who opened the door.

"Well don't wait out there, my dears;" said Alice, "it looks as though we're in for a downpour!"

"Eric!" she shouted back into the lounge. "We have visitors!"

Alice closed the door after them, "This is nice; we haven't seen you two in a while."

"Eric!" she repeated, more sternly.

Inky's uncle had been dozing in front of the TV, hands laced across his paunch, "But the News is on," he said groggily.

"Never mind that; come and say hello!"

Eric slipped on his tartan slippers and entered the hallway in time to catch Rose and Ross handing over their coats. As always, he marvelled at the pair, who despite being brother and sister, were almost identical: both were short in stature and sported short, brown, bobbed hair, and both had the same bright eyes, same button noses and the same scattering of freckles across crab-apple cheeks.

"Well, if it isn't the Berry twins!" said Eric. "Nice to see you again. Inky's in his room. He's been in there since he came home from school. Go on up!"

"I'll just go and fetch some biscuits," added Alice.

"Thanks, Mrs Garner," replied the twins.

Watching them head towards Inky's room, Alice felt a surge of relief. She was always happy when her nephew had visitors; she worried about the time he spent alone.

Childless themselves, no couple could have offered more love and support to their nephew. Bringing a withdrawn teenager into a quiet, suburban home in an isolated and dreary coastal town was not without its challenges, but the Garners were determined to make the best of it. "Family's family," said Alice, and she made it her business to make up for what had been taken from the boy.

On entering Inky's room, the twins couldn't help feeling that they were passing from summer into midwinter; his bedroom contrasted so sharply with the rest of the Garners' home. Everything in it appeared to be a different shade of black: a large metal bed with dark grey, cotton bedding dominated the space, its headboard wrought from strands of iron which wound upwards like galvanised ivy; the curtains, closed to black out the dusk's arrival, were of charcoal-coloured crushed velvet; and pale grey candles set into wall-mounted holders sent flickering shadows dancing across black-painted walls, as wax slowly melted down to form stalactites beneath.

The detective's desk was positioned just to the right of the window. On top of this sat a notebook and a black, touch-key typewriter.

Inky had been waiting for them, pacing the floor with long strides. After a cursory greeting, he proceeded to outline the case of the caretaker's keys.

Meanwhile, the pair made themselves comfortable: Ross placed the miniature crow onto Inky's desk and then laid back on the bed with his hands tucked behind his head, while Rose sat on the chair at the desk. Both listened carefully.

Several minutes lapsed before Inky reached his conclusion, "The thief who stole the master copies of the school's keys is one of four suspects: Spud Barton, Candy Sugarcane, Wilfred Whitkirk or Crispin Merridew."

"Not Crispin, surely?" said Ross. "I can't see him breaking school rules, let alone stealing."

"Yes," said Inky, "I'm interested to hear your views. What would motivate someone to take the school keys?"

"Perhaps it's just someone messing around," suggested Rose, "you know, playing a prank or trying to impress someone? The school's full of show-offs."

"Or they could have been stolen to blackmail Fred?" suggested Ross.

Rose was struck by a sudden thought: "Candy could have taken them to get into Miss Peters' office," she said. "There must be hundreds of pounds of her confiscated make-up locked in there."

Ross laughed, "Candy's so brainless she could just have picked them up without knowing what she was doing."

"Seriously, though," Rose said, "isn't the thief most likely to be Spud Barton because ..."

"... because causing trouble is what Spud does?" said Ross.

Explanations exhausted, the twins sat back, while the young investigator continued to pace the room, deep in thought. The twins followed his movement in silence, heads sweeping to and fro like spectators at a slow-motion tennis match. Finally, he came to a halt.

"We have just over two days left in which to find the keys before the Snake discovers Fred's negligence," said Inky. "Tomorrow, without arousing suspicion, we will place each of the four suspects under surveillance, noting anything unusual. We will also need to search their bags in the hope that one of them may still have the keys about their person, but we must only attempt this if it can be done without the investigation being compromised. Your chief role is to observe and report back."

"And if we spot something important?" asked Ross.

"Let me know immediately," Inky replied. "Keep your eyes and ears open at all times. Should Fred make contact via Dukes during registration, I'll share anything relevant, but we must be discreet. No one, but ourselves, Fred and Dukes, knows about this."

"Apart from the thief," said Rose.

"Of course," said Inky, "Rose, I want you to follow Candy tomorrow. You share music with her Lesson Two and PE Lesson Five. Make sure you have her in your sight. And Ross, I'd like you to do the same for Crispin. He's a second-year so you won't be in any of his lessons, but you can follow him at break and lunchtime, and I need you to attend Drama Club with him after school. It's held in the Drama Studio with Miss Birkin."

Ross pulled a face. He hated drama, and 'Flouncy' Birkin was his least favourite teacher.

Inky continued undaunted, "To assist with the surveillance, I've made copies of both Candy's and Crispin's timetables." He removed two sheets of paper from his desk drawer and passed them over. "These will tell you where they ought to be during lesson times, both on Tuesday and Wednesday."

"How did you get hold of these?" asked Rose.

A smile played across Inky's lips, "I arranged for Miss Cartwright to leave the Reception and then made duplicates from the master copy while she was away."

"You're amazing!" said Ross.

Inky continued, ignoring the praise, "Well, if there are no further questions, we'll meet back here at six tomorrow evening, okay?"

"Okay," came the joint reply.

"Enjoy Drama Club, Ross!" said Inky with a flicker of mischief.

CHAPTER FIVE –
CANDY TRAIL

On Tuesday morning, Candy Sugarcane wafted through the school gates fifteen minutes late and arrived at registration coated in her usual layers of foundation, powder and rouge. Peregrine Dukes looked up at her in disbelief, "Candy Sugarcane, please report to Miss Peters immediately! You're late again, and you know that wearing make-up is against school rules."

Candy sauntered out of the room, and immediately afterwards, Rose piped up, "Mr Dukes, I need to see Miss Peters too."

"Do you?"

"Yes, Miss Peters would like to discuss my options."

"Why? I thought you were happy with what you've chosen."

"I want to review them," said Rose.

"Very well," sighed Dukes, "but afterwards please go straight to your first lesson."

"Yes, Sir. Thank you."

Rose hurried after Candy, who was meandering on delicately balanced heels towards the Head of Year's office, pausing to check her appearance in any reflective surface she passed: windows, door knobs, laminated posters. Indeed, Candy was so preoccupied with all this checking that she never once suspected she was being followed, and by the time she entered Miss Peters' office, Rose had completely caught up and managed to slip into the only available hiding place – behind a life-size, bronze statue celebrating former pupil Lionel Roebuck, a pioneer of the frozen waffle industry.

Inside her office, Miss Peters was feeling frazzled. The stresses of school, even just three weeks in, were already taking their toll, and the sight of Candy pouting in front of her, twirling long strands of hair around her fingers, did nothing to improve her mood. "Miss Sugarcane, you know very well that make-up is not permitted in this school."

Candy opened her mouth to protest, but Miss Peters had already thumped a plastic packet down onto the desk, "Here are some wipes. I want it all removed!"

"But, Miss, these wipes are for bloomin' insect bites!" said Candy, studying the packet.

"They're all-purpose wipes," said Miss Peters. "I don't want any arguments, just get scrubbing!"

Candy began sulkily removing each coat of colour, her eyes blazing with impotent rage.

"Thank you," said Miss Peters. "Now, open your bag!"

"Aawww! Why, Miss?" bleated Candy.

"You know why."

Candy, realising that further protest was pointless, hoisted her school bag onto the desk.

Outside the office, Rose Berry peered closer through the slightly open doorway as, one by one, Candy produced a cosmetics counter's worth of products: face powder, eye-liner, strawberry-scented perfume, blusher, mascara, lip-liner, foundation, concealer, hairspray, and a heart-shaped hairbrush.

"Everything!" demanded Miss Peters.

Candy delved deeper into her bag and, mouth quivering, fished out a single tube of lipstick.

Rose was disappointed not to see Fred's keys among the items piled on the desk, but before she could scrutinise everything, Miss Peters had unlocked her office drawer and swept everything into it – everything except the lipstick, which had rolled to the edge of the desk.

"Thank you, Miss Sugarcane," she said, locking the drawer

and returning its key to her trouser pocket. "Go back to your class now. You may retrieve your belongings at the end of term, provided that you're a *model* student between now and then."

At that moment, Miss Peters caught a glimpse of Rose, "Miss Berry?" she said, "Is something wrong?"

"Erm, no Miss," said Rose, stepping away from the statue and into the doorway, "I was just, erm, on my way to maths. Can't be late. Bye!"

****

Rose spent the rest of the day shadowing Candy. They had two lessons in common: music during Period Two, and PE during Period Five, which should have made the task easier, but towards the end of music, Candy gave Rose the slip. "Miss, I need to go to the loo!" she said.

"Very well, but be quick!" replied Miss Sheldon.

Watching Candy leave, limp school bag in hand, Rose began to panic. She asked to be excused too, but Miss Sheldon held firm, "You know the rules, Rose. Only one person goes to the toilet at a time. You can go when Candy returns."

But Candy did not return, at least not for some time, and when she did, there was a smug grin plastered across her pallid face, and her school bag was limp and flabby no more.

Immediately after the lesson, Rose spotted something else. Tailing from a safe distance, she watched her target disappear into the senior girls' toilet, where she remained for the rest of the break. When Candy re-emerged, she was fully made up. Her tangerine complexion, cherry lips and black-lined eyes had all reappeared. From somewhere, Candy had managed to get her hands on a whole array of cosmetics.

During PE too, Candy made it difficult for Rose to stay close to her. In typical sullen fashion, she refused point-blank to get changed for hockey, telling the newly qualified Miss Hassell that she had no intention of taking part in any activity that might risk breaking her teeth. So instead, Candy opted to sit in the Sports Hall alone and watch a recording of England's 1966 World Cup victory, making a transcript of the commentary.

****

Rose was beginning to think that her day's surveillance had been a waste of time, but just as everyone was leaving for home, something strange happened: Rose was following Candy out of school from a safe distance, hidden amongst the crush of escaping students, when suddenly her suspect came to an abrupt halt outside Fred Varley's Maintenance Room.

Rose ducked behind the school minibus and watched as Candy reached out and knocked on Fred's door: a single, dainty knock. There was no answer. Next, Candy slapped against it with the flat of her hand. There was a brief pause before Fred appeared. From her vantage point, Rose saw Fred's expression sour and he and Candy seemingly exchange heated words.

By the time the crowd of departing students had thinned, Fred's door had closed, leaving Candy standing in front of it alone. Rose noted that for the first time that day Candy looked vulnerable: her shoulders were slumped and her face uncharacteristically pale, but it was fleeting, and after a few moments, she tossed back her hair, swung her school bag over her shoulder and set off for home.

"Now that's interesting," Rose thought, "I wonder what Inky will make of that?"

CHAPTER SIX –
THE CRIME SCENE

During registration, Inky threaded his way between rows of badly positioned tables and stood before Mr Dukes' desk. A discreet nod from the form tutor told him everything he needed to know. In a blink, he was on his way, striding along empty corridors towards the Science Laboratory. It was time to find out what Wilfred Whitkirk knew about Fred's missing keys.

Inky's boots rapped on the tiled floor as he moved onwards. He swept past several dusty glass cases containing botanical samples and past a display board, which hailed second-year Melanie Pringle as 'Biologist of the Month' – it had been hanging there since February.

Inky arrived at the Science Lab and unhooked his rucksack. As he reached out to knock, the door swung open, and there stood Ray Day, Blinkton's Head of Science.

In general, Blinkton's pupils were wary of Day – a giant of a man, bald-headed and barrel-chested, with shirt buttons straining to contain his sheer bulk. He was friendly enough, jovial at times, but tended to be overbearing. He also liked to address students as if they were his mates, thinking they'd find his chumminess endearing; they didn't.

"Ink-o!" he boomed. "How can I help?"

"I was hoping to see Mr Whitkirk, Sir."

At the mention of the Technician's name, a black look crossed Day's face.

Inky continued, "I need to ask his advice about my science project, Sir."

The bluntness in Day's tone was apparent, "Sorry, Ink-o, he's not here. Rang in about half an hour ago. Said he wouldn't be in today."

"Isn't that unusual?"

"Possibly, but nothing for you to worry about. He'll be back tomorrow for sure. Can I be of assistance?"

Inky shrank back. "I don't think so, Sir," he said.

"What's your project? Anything engineering-related? You know I've built my own racing car – a dragster. Fast as lightning she is. Burnin' up the drag strip! Red, amber, green and go, go, GO!"

Inky was unimpressed, "Thanks for the offer, Sir, but the project isn't related to cars or anything mechanical."

"Okey-dokey, Ink-o. See you around, dude."

"Thanks, Sir," replied Inky flatly.

The laboratory door slammed shut with a force that tested its hinges.

With time scarce, Whitkirk going AWOL was a serious problem. Inky decided to use what little remained of registration for a different purpose: he immediately cut back across the school, hoping that the scene of the crime might reveal a few secrets.

****

The fact that there were so few items in the Reflection Room made Inky's task easier. An initial glance confirmed that everything appeared to be in its rightful place: Harmony Tent, carpet, table, record player, scatter cushions. Coloured lamps were set around the edges of the room throwing up pools of orange, red and blue light onto the white walls. One lamp wasn't working and lay on its side.

Inky immediately focused his attention on the table at the far end of the room – the spot from where Fred's keys had gone missing. At first glance, he could see nothing remarkable: a metal-framed table, etched with graffiti, on top of which sat a telephone, two speakers and the record player itself. Then, just as he was about to turn his attention towards the Harmony Tent, a tiny pinprick of light glinted at him from behind a table leg. Closer inspection revealed a small item of jewellery trapped between it and the skirting board. Inky plucked it free and held it up for inspection; it was a cufflink – expensive-looking, comprising a single diamond encased in a silver mounting.

The young detective renewed his search in earnest, running his hands beneath the underside of the table in a sweeping motion so that not an inch remained untouched. His fingers soon alighted on another small object, one fixed there with duct tape. Deft fingers picked at the edges of this until the item became loose and dropped into his palm. It was an electrical component no bigger than a thumbnail.

"Interesting," thought Inky, placing his second find carefully into his coat pocket, alongside the first. He then approached the giant tent that dominated the room, swiftly unzipped it and stooped inside.

Inside, an additional set of cushions had been strewn across the tent's floor. Inky shook each of these in turn, looking for evidence, before examining the inner sides. He brushed down its sloping walls, its side-pockets and finally smoothed out all the wrinkles in the canvas floor. Suddenly, his hands alighted on another object: something small, sharp and metallic; and as he slid it out from among the folds of the material, he allowed himself the faintest of smiles, "Now this is something," he thought.

It was a key – a rather elaborate-looking key. The detective hastily placed it with his other discoveries, and then froze at the sound of the Reflection Room door being flung open. No longer alone and trapped, a knot formed in the pit of Inky's stomach. He held his breath and silently lay down. From his hiding place, Inky used a finger to fashion the tiniest of spy-holes at the base of the tent flap and peered through cautiously.

The intruder loped over to the table like a grizzly bear and began to paw at its top in a state of agitation. Not finding what he was after, he then knelt to search underneath. Because of his bulk, the man's shirt came loose during his frantic search, its tail flapping down loosely over his corduroy trousers.

The man's frustration finally spilled over, "You've got it coming, Whitt-o!" he growled.

Inky watched in silence as the oversized figure heaved back onto his feet using the table as support, smoothed down his clothes and departed. The door slammed behind him with a force that caused the sides of the Harmony Tent to quiver.

Inky breathed out slowly, relieved, but reluctant to move. Finally, he crept over to the door, pulled it open a centimetre at a time until he was certain there was no one there other than the clusters of vacant-looking students dragging themselves to class. Only then did Inky ease himself out into the corridor and quickly lose himself among the crowd.

As the detective lumbered along with his adopted bunch of stragglers, his thoughts began to spin: "Three pieces of evidence, including one of Fred's missing keys. And with Whitkirk absent, it was time to focus on another suspect: my date with Spud Barton has just been brought forward."

Instead of heading towards Science, Inky doubled back towards Miss Peters' office.

CHAPTER SEVEN –
THE DRAMA UNFOLDS

Ross Berry was confused: in many ways Crispin Merridew was the most straightforward suspect to investigate, but in others he was the most challenging. Crispin's habits and movements were entirely predictable, but being a second-year, he was not in Ross's year group and that made him difficult to tail. Most of Ross's surveillance was therefore confined to break times, and these were nearly always cut short as Crispin set off to all his lessons early. Whatever the class, he was there ahead of time, with his homework carefully laid out for his teacher's approval.

"It's not natural," thought Ross, and he did not wonder that the young brainbox tended to sit alone.

Lunchtime proved equally unenlightening for Ross. As English came to an end, he offered to take the class's copies of *Lord of the Flies* back to the storeroom for Chalky Whittle. This enabled him to slip away early in the hope of catching Crispin as he left his textiles class.

Ross arrived just in time to see the door fly open and a tangle of skinny-limbed students pouring out on their way to the dining hall. Crispin was the only student not among them; he'd stayed behind to ask for extra help with his embroidery. Mrs Morris patiently demonstrated a complicated stitch again – a smile fixed on her face, her mind on the slabs of apple pie fast disappearing from the dining hall.

With the stitch mastered, Crispin finally departed. The speed at which he travelled meant that Ross struggled to keep up. If Crispin had been the least bit observant, he could have easily spotted Ross racing after him, red-faced and runny-nosed, but he was oblivious.

Ross finally slowed to a crawl and left Crispin to race off. "I can guess where he's going, anyway," he thought.

****

Ross was taken aback by the scene that greeted him inside the dimly lit Reflection Room. Groups of the school's most vulnerable pupils stood around amiably or lay sprawled out on the floor cushions. Everyone was talking and laughing and offering one another packets of crisps, chocolate bars, cans of pop, pear drops, liquorice bootlaces, sherbet fountains and walnut whips. The mood among the gathering was refreshingly pleasant and sociable – harmonious even. The sound of laughter and idle chatter bubbled up over the *Beatles Songbook on Panpipes*, which played in the background.

Sitting at the desk from which Fred's keys had been taken was Old Hazel, the lunchtime supervisor – a plump woman with the throaty laugh of a hardened smoker. She was dressed in a plain, white dress, over which she wore a blue tabard, and her hair was grey and wiry, sprouting randomly from her scalp. But Old Hazel's most distinctive feature was positioned on the end of her chin – a bulbous wart, the size of a grape, which hung from the underside of her jaw as though it had been stuck on with glue. This was crowned with a cluster of hairs that shot outwards like pins in a pincushion.

Old Hazel immediately identified Ross as a newcomer and beckoned him over, "Not seen you in the Reflection Room before, my dear. What's your name?"

"Erm, erm, Trevor," spluttered Ross, "Cushion. I'm Trevor Cushion."

"Anything I can help you with, Trevor?"

Ross dropped his voice to a whisper, "I came to see Crispin. Is he in the Harmony Tent?"

"He is," said Old Hazel warmly. "Why do you want to see him?"

Ross continued nervously, "I'm concerned about him, that's all. He seems to be a bit of a loner, and I wondered if he was in some kind of trouble."

"No, I think he just wants a bit of peace."

"Really?" said Ross, trying to avoid looking at Old Hazel's chin.

"That's what this room's for. Crispin comes here most lunchtimes. Sometimes he likes to sit inside the Harmony Tent; sometimes outside," she paused, "on a *cushion*, Trevor."

Ross blushed, but continued, "What does he *do*, inside the Harmony Tent?"

"Puzzles," said Old Hazel simply. "Inside that satchel of his, Crispin has all kinds of puzzles. He loves 'em: crosswords, quizzes, word searches. They keep his brain ticking over."

Ross cast his eye around the room. He suddenly felt very hot.

Old Hazel thought that 'Trevor' must have something troubling him. "Sometimes, Crispin likes to have a chat with me. We all need a friendly ear now and again, don't we?"

"Erm, yes," said Ross, looking down. He felt that he was making some progress with Inky's task, but a bigger part of him knew that he was making a complete fool of himself. "When Crispin speaks to you, Miss, what does he say?"

Old Hazel's eyebrows creased.

Ross began to flounder. "I mean, is there anything he's particularly worried about? Anything which might be troubling him?"

Old Hazel leant forwards, establishing eye contact, "Let's just say that if little Crispin is feeling troubled, it's nothing to do with school."

But before Ross could answer, something unexpected happened. An eruption of jeers and cries from outside suddenly sliced through the idle chatter. The atmosphere darkened in an instant.

The Harmony Tent remained tightly zipped.

"Nothing to worry about, everyone," said Old Hazel, huffing up onto her feet. "There's a bit of a kerfuffle going on in the yard. I'll have it all sorted out in no time. Just wait here, and I'll be back in two shakes of a lamb's wool."

From the far corner, two second-years smiled at Ross. Usually Ross wouldn't associate with pupils two years below him, but he was on a mission and so decided to approach the cheery looking pair, "Hi there," he said. "Do either of you know Crispin Merridew?"

****

At the end of lunch time, the tent's zip finally opened, and Crispin crept out, wiped his spectacles, and ran off, whizzing down the Performing Arts corridor once more. Ross decided not to follow. He knew Crispin's movements – French, then maths and then the dreaded Drama Club. He said goodbye to his new friends with a feeling of guilt; he didn't like deceiving people.

"See you around, Trev," they said in unison.

Old Hazel added, "I hope to see you in here again, Master Cushion. You're welcome any time."

****

At four o'clock, Ross looked on enviously as packs of children scampered through the school gates and disappeared down Wordsworth Drive. Slowly, he dragged his feet in the opposite direction towards the Drama Studio and Flouncy Birkin.

Seeing Ross framed in the Studio entrance, Sally Birkin's face formed itself into a question, "Master Berry? What a pleasant surprise! Are you passing, or are you intending to join us?"

Ross stared at Flouncy's beetroot-coloured lipstick and trademark beret, "I just fancied, you know, trying out a bit of drama," he mumbled, quickly scanning the room to make sure Crispin was there.

"Excellent, Monsieur Berry!" trilled Flouncy. "Pray enter from stage left. Fetch a chair and join our merry band of thespians."

Ross collected a chair from beneath a mirror framed by lightbulbs and dragged it across the sprung flooring to join the rest of the group. It was then that he noticed, to his horror, that all the participants in the Drama Club – other than himself and Crispin – were girls, and mostly first-years at that. They giggled to one other as he sat down. Crispin, sitting opposite, seemed perfectly at ease.

"In this session, we'll be exploring conflict," announced Flouncy. "Conflict, fear and tension."

"Great!" thought Ross. "Just what I need – more tension."

"Right," said Flouncy. "Pairs, everyone! I'd like you to partner up for tonight's main activity."

"This is it," thought Ross, "my chance to find out something useful."

"Hi there!" he said rushing over to Crispin, "Do you mind if I work with you?"

"Fine," Crispin replied chirpily. "It's nice to have another boy in the Club. You should audition in the school production. Rehearsals begin after Christmas."

"Everybody!" interrupted Flouncy, "One, two, three, and hush!"

In the silence that followed, Ross felt an uncomfortable prickle which started at his temples and ran down his spine.

"Working in pairs, I'd like you to present a piece of work entitled 'My deepest fears'. I want you to draw on your emotions to create a meaningful performance based on your own anxieties."

Flouncy began to stalk the room as she spoke, her blouse billowing out behind her like a parachute. "I want you to capture the essence of fear. To achieve this, you'll need to *commune* with your character in an artistic truth that exposes your very soul, then you'll need to deconstruct that truth and reconstruct it into a raw and meaningful performance, and you've got ten minutes!"

Ross dragged a shirt-cuff across his brow. He wasn't at all sure what Flouncy was talking about so he waited for Crispin to take the lead.

"Right," said Crispin, brightly, "we're exploring phobias, so what are you most afraid of?"

Ross became evasive, "I think I'd be more comfortable if we used your fears instead, Crispin. I'm a bit new to all this."

Crispin's eyes widened, "How did you know my name?"

"Well, didn't Miss call you Crispin?"

"No."

"I must have picked it up around school." Ross felt a bead of sweat trickle down his back.

"Eight minutes left!" shouted Flouncy, her heavy jewellery clacking like castanets.

Ross looked around the studio, gripped by panic. Around him a frenzy of girls were busily practising their dramas. They gestured, pointed and generally heaved one another about.

"Come on, Crispin!" urged Ross, "We haven't got much time. Tell me what *your* deepest fears are."

Crispin skimmed a hand across his fringe, "Well, I'm scared of failing exams," he said. "And I was nervous about learning Latin too, before I realised how simple it was."

"We're all nervous about those things. Is there anything that frightens you in particular?"

"Kids pick on me," said Crispin. I don't know why, but they do. Last Friday, Bridie McMuffin and Kristy Gee attacked me in cookery. They flicked cake mix over me and hit me with a spoon. They thought it was funny."

Ross loosened his tie, "What about keys?" he asked.

Crispin looked puzzled, "Why would anyone be afraid of keys?"

"Well, what about locks?" spluttered Ross.

"Fear of locked doors is a possibility, I suppose – fear of being trapped, or something lurking behind a locked door."

"Three minutes!" yelled Flouncy.

"I'm quite scared right now!" Ross blurted. "We've nothing to show Flouncy. I haven't got any ideas. I'm not very creative. I don't like performing … I mean, I haven't … I've never liked drama."

"Why have you come to Drama Club then?" asked Crispin.

Flouncy's voice sliced the air like a guillotine, "Everybody! One, two, three, and hush! Time's up! Well done everyone, I'm looking forward to seeing your *masterpieces*. Please, can we clear a performance space? And we'll see what are your," she dropped her voice and added a spooky effect, "deepest fears!"

Over the next ten minutes, members of Blinkton's Drama Club presented their work: some pieces were emotional (about clowns and drowning), some were thought-provoking (about poverty and abandonment), and one was funny (concerning an alien with flatulence). Then came the moment Ross was dreading.

"Right," said Flouncy, "who hasn't performed?"

Ross sank as far back into his chair as its hard plastic allowed.

"Ah yes! It's our two menfolk. Take it away, Messieurs Merridew and Berry!"

Crispin shot up and arranged a table and chairs in the middle of the performance space, while Ross hovered behind.

Under his breath Crispin whispered, "We'll just have to make it up as we go along – improvisation it's called – you just sit on that chair, smile and say lots of nice things about me, okay?"

"Ladies and gentlemen," Crispin announced, grandly. "Well, just ladies actually, our performance is entitled 'Parents' Evening'. My personal fear is how my father might react at parents' evening. I shall be playing my father, Lord Marmaduke Merridew, Crown Court Judge and Head of the School Governors. My new friend, Ross, will be playing my form tutor, Miss Aries."

A round of giggles bubbled up from the audience causing Ross to turn the colour of Flouncy's lipstick.

Crispin walked to the edge of the performance area then spun around and re-entered in character. Crispin, as Lord Merridew, was no longer the lonely misfit who buzzed around school with his head tilted towards the floor. Chest puffed out, shoulders back, and eyes squeezed into thin slits, he exuded an air of pomposity and menace.

'Lord Merridew' approached the table. He looked down at 'Miss Aries', brimming with self-importance. "Miss Aquarius," he boomed, "sorry I'm late, I had a pressing engagement with the judiciary. Pesky felon received a life sentence. I am Lord Merridew by the way. How do you do?"

Ross accepted the hand thrust towards him, surprised at the strength in its grip.

"I'm here to discuss my son's progress."

"Erm, yes, Crispin ..."

In a whisper, Crispin interrupted, "Ask me to sit down!"

"What?"

"It's parents' evening, and I'm still standing. Miss Aries

would ask parents to take a seat. Come on, Ross, start acting!"

Ross took a deep breath, "Lord Merridew, how good of you to come. Please, take a seat," he said.

The audience tittered at Ross's attempt to mimic one of their teachers. Pleased at having provoked a reaction, he could feel himself growing in confidence.

"Thank you, Miss Aquarius." Crispin sat down, planted his elbows on the table and leaned in, "Now, if you'd be so good as to inform me of my son's progress?"

"Yes, of course," said Ross, fumbling in Crispin's satchel as if in search of paperwork.

"Come on!" Crispin yelled suddenly, the anger in his eyes magnified through his spectacles, "What's the matter with you? Is my son in your form, or not? Do you, or do you not, have the results of his assessments?"

Flouncy's mouth fell open. The entire front row of the audience recoiled in shock.

Ross stopped acting; his fear was now genuine, "Of course, of course I do, Lord Merridew," he spluttered. "It's just …"

Crispin spat, "Come on, Aquarius! How is my son doing at this school?"

"He's, he's doing very well," Ross floundered, his voice taking on a higher pitch, "very well indeed."

Frightened eyes looked across at Flouncy, but Crispin was

caught up in the moment. 'Lord Merridew' gripped hold of the table, knuckles whitening. He stood up, leaned over and yelled, "He's doing well, is he? Well?"

"Yes, he's ... he's lovely," flapped Ross, instantly regretting his choice of phrase. "He's doing very well in all of his subjects."

"Well? *Well!* 'Well' is not good enough!"

Crispin's voice rose to a steady thunder, "'Well' is below the standard that I expect from my son. My son is in bed by eight every night to ensure he'll be refreshed and ready to excel the next day. Doing 'well' is a slur on both *him* and on *my* reputation."

"Lord Merridew, I don't think you understand—"

"No, Aquarius, I don't think *you* understand. To do *well* is nothing. Nothing at all. It's an abomination! I'll be having words with Crispin when I get home. My son was not brought up to do 'well'!"

Crispin was now completely red-faced. Flecks of spittle dotted the table top in front of him. With a roar, his grip on the table tightened and he flipped his arms upwards. The table soared into the air and spiralled for a moment before landing upside-down on the sprung flooring.

BANG! The sound of wood splintering echoed around the Drama Studio.

Crispin paused for a beat, a tableau of fury. Then, coming

back to life, he wrestled his satchel from Ross's grip and stormed off, raging down the corridor.

The audience was silent. Ross sat alone on stage, dry-mouthed and desperately wanting to be somewhere else.

Then, after a long pause, Lucy Spragg broke the mood with a single clap. Dawn Riss and Shelvey Pomm looked at one another before joining in.

Clap, clap, clap.

Karen Rex followed suit, as did Michelle Toshack, until a surge of applause erupted. Cheers, whistles and screams filled the room: "Marvellous!" "Tremendous!" "Bravo!"

Rita Hamer, hoping for a lead role in the school production, tried to impress, "What a *tour-de-force* that was, Miss, a real *coup-de-theatre!*"

One by one, the Drama Club members turned to face the door, awaiting Crispin's reappearance, but Crispin Merridew did not return.

"What a finale!" said Flouncy, finally finding her voice, "I must congratulate young Merridew when I ..." she looked at the door expectantly before turning away, "when I see him tomorrow. He's obviously ... Yes, I'll see him tomorrow. And well done to you, too, Master Berry. You were the perfect foil ... foil to the emotionally charged intensity which Master Merridew brought to the *role* of his father."

Flouncy rose to her feet, "That's it, everyone. See you next week, and don't forget, we have auditions! There will be a part for everyone. I think you'd make an excellent pantomime dame, Master Berry."

"Perhaps, Miss," Ross replied in a non-committal tone.

****

With the session over and Crispin gone, Ross was in no hurry to hang around. He scooped up his belongings and shot out of school, relieved that the ordeal was over. On the way home, he zipped his coat against the wind and reflected to himself, "I was worried I'd have nothing to report back to Inky. Well, that's just changed!"

CHAPTER EIGHT –
THE BIG WIND-UP

Once Inky had conducted his search of the Reflection Room, he turned his attention to Spud Barton. To find out what he needed, he would have to get Spud rattled, really rattled, and he knew exactly how to achieve this.

Inky made his way to Miss Peters' office, knocked on the door and strode in grandly. "I've come to see you about a serious matter, Miss," he announced, immediately catching sight of a tube of lipstick abandoned on her desk.

"What is it, Inky?" she snapped, struggling to free her over-large bottom from the chair. "Can't this wait? The bell's gone, and I'm supposed to be teaching."

"It's William Barton," said Inky, flopping down on a chair, and slipping the lipstick into his pocket.

Miss Peters sighed, "You have one minute. What has he been

up to this time?"

"It's bad, Miss. He's *selling!*"

"Selling what?"

Inky continued his fabrication, "He's defrauding the school, Miss, undercutting the tuck shop. Barton brings in carrier bags full of stuff to sell in the playground."

"Yes, but what is this *stuff* he's selling?"

"Cans of pop, crisps, biscuits, chocolate bars, noodle snack pots – that kind of thing."

"Come on, Inky, *noodle snack pots?* It's hardly the Great Train Robbery."

Inky realised that he'd have to up his game: "Plus cigarettes, lighters and fireworks."

There was a moment's pause.

"Oh," groaned Miss Peters, "that's different."

"He's making a fortune, Miss. There's one price for us older kids, then he doubles it for second- and third-years, and the first-years have to pay treble."

Miss Peters massaged her temples wearily.

"And some of the first-years are *pressured* into buying things. I saw Barton force Alison Everett into buying a peanut bar, and she's—"

"Allergic to nuts!"

"Precisely. And even worse," he dropped his voice, "the

reason why he's making such a huge profit is because ..."

"Go on," said Miss Peters.

"Because he has no outlay whatsoever. He steals everything from Higgison's Newsagents."

"No!"

"Yes! Barton threatens Mr Higgison every morning before school. The poor old soul's terrified. He just hands over whatever Barton demands without question. He's scamming mountains of goods, Miss. He's even stealing the carrier bags to put them in."

Miss Peters brought her hand up to her mouth. "This is serious, Inky. Something needs to be done right away!"

"Yes, but what about your Year Two class?" said Inky, clambering to his feet. "Perhaps I should bring this to the attention of the Snake?"

"The Snake!" said Miss Peters alarmed. "I don't want her slithering around my year group. She's worked up enough about some maths prize."

"In that case, I could ..." said Inky, before shaking his head. "No, sorry, forget it."

"What could you do?" urged Miss Peters, wanting to rise, but finding herself still attached to her chair.

Inky steepled his hands beneath his chin, "I was just going to suggest that I could help you out."

"How?" asked Miss Peters.

"Spud has Woodwork during Lesson One with Mr Foreshaw. I could go to Room D3 on your behalf, Miss, and confiscate his school bag for you. Then I could send him down to the Isolation Unit for you to deal with later."

Miss Peters reached for a pad on which to scribble a note of consent, tore off a leaf of paper and was about to hand it over when she stopped. Something felt wrong. The Head of Year thought hard, struggling to recover a memory buried deep in her mind – something about a letter, something from the Council she was supposed to deal with, something in Stevens' file.

"Is there a problem, Miss?" asked Inky.

"No," she finally replied, as if talking to herself. "It'll come back to me. It's just something I had to look at in your file. I'll check it out later." And, with a shrug, she handed the note to Inky.

Inky was a mask of indifference, revealing nothing of the heavy feeling that had settled in the pit of his stomach. "I'll be off then," he said.

****

"William Barton!" yelled 'Polo Mint' Foreshaw at the thick-set brute at the back of his Woodwork Room. "Give your bag to Inky Stevens! You're to go to the Isolation Unit now! Do not pass go! Do not collect two hundred pounds!"

Barton looked up, hammer in hand, his muscular arm poised in mid-air, and considered whether it was time to stop raining down a series of killer blows onto the defenceless nail quivering below. He hesitated, looked down at the delicate piece of metal, then decided to batter it anyway:

THWACK!

"What's this about?" he asked.

"No idea, Barton," said Foreshaw, "Miss Peters' orders. Just get along to the Isolation Unit. Inky will accompany you to make sure you don't get lost."

"Miss Peters' orders?" said Spud, "I've not done nothing!"

THWACK!

"Ask 'Grim Reaper' Stevens here on your way."

"What if I say 'no'?"

THWACK!

"Then it looks like our next task will be to make you a coffin."

Spud raised his hammer once more, glaring at Foreshaw, then at Inky, then back at Foreshaw. Realising that he had no option, he lowered his work tool, untied his apron and grabbed hold of his bag.

"Leave the bag for Stevens!" ordered Foreshaw.

Spud stared his teacher out, before finally allowing his bag to drop down onto the scattering of wood shavings covering the floor. Inky, who had not taken his eyes off Spud since he'd arrived, noted that his bag appeared empty. Certainly, there was no tell-tale jangling of keys as it struck the floor.

Spud strode out of Room D3, leaving Inky to gather up his bag. The investigator duly seized it and slung it over his shoulder before setting off in pursuit.

Spud smiled as he made his way across the yard, waving at all the students he could see across the playground in 'Brylcreem' Mountjoy's Geography lesson. For once, he knew he hadn't done anything wrong. He also knew that, even though it might take time, he'd be able to wring some sort of apology out of someone eventually.

****

The Isolation Unit was a specially adapted classroom, located opposite the staff room. It was an educational cell designed to segregate Blinkton's most challenging students from the rest of the school. Inside, several troublemakers could sit working within specially designed booths facing the wall, while members of staff watched over them on a rota. That Tuesday it was the turn of Blinkton's Deputy Head, Mike Bennett, and Spud was his first arrival.

Before disappearing inside, Spud turned to Inky: "If I find that being yanked out of woodwork has anything to do with you, Stevens, you are dead meat!"

As soon as Spud was gone, Inky immediately began to inspect his bag. He unzipped it, and thrust his hands deep inside, checking its pockets, and turning it inside out just to make doubly sure, but there was nothing there; Spud's bag was empty: no exercise books, no pen, nothing.

Inky resolved to investigate further. He stepped into the Isolation Unit and approached Mr Bennett, who was seated at the front, almost hidden from view behind an enormous pile of maths exercise books. "Morning, Sir," he said, "May I return this school bag to William Barton?"

"Of course, Stevens," Bennett replied, "he's over there."

Inky walked over to Spud, and leaned in close, keeping his voice low, "Here's your bag. It would appear that you've forgotten your school books."

Barton sneered, "What's inside my bag is exactly what I need for this school."

"I agree, William, or should I say, Wilma?"

Spud growled in confusion, "What you sayin', Stevens? Whatever stunt you're trying to pull with Peters won't work. I'm gonna tell that old thunder-butt that you set me up."

"Oh, I wouldn't do that, Wilma. You see, your bag wasn't quite empty, was it?"

"What?"

Inky set Candy's lipstick down onto Spud's desk. The golden

cylinder spun on its base and gradually circled to a standstill. Spud immediately clenched his fist around it and rammed it into his trouser pocket. "What are you up to, Stevens?" he said, grabbing hold of Inky's lapels and yanking him forwards in an action quiet enough so as not to disturb the preoccupied Deputy. Nose to nose with his tormentor, Spud snarled, "We both know that lipstick isn't mine, Stevens!"

"But the rest of the school doesn't," said Inky. "By the way, I'm not sure that pillar-box red is your colour. I've always thought of you as more of a *peach* man myself."

Spud hissed, "You're dead, Stevens. As dead as a ..." he struggled for the appropriate word, "something that's really dead!"

"We need to discuss this further, Barton. See you by the bike sheds at twelve forty-five."

"Fine," snarled Spud, releasing his grip. "You're not going to get away with this, Stevens."

Inky turned and added, "See you there then, Sweetheart," before moving off.

****

That lunchtime, an enormous gang of snotty-nosed kids turned their backs on bangers and mash and raced over to the bike sheds, buzzing with anticipation: Spud Barton versus Inky Stevens; Neanderthal thug versus black-coated weirdo. News of the fight had passed quickly on the school grapevine; the chant *'fight, fight, fight'* pulsing through tiny minds. It seemed that almost the entire school had scurried along, clamouring for a front-row seat.

Like a prize fighter, Spud emerged from the RE Department with an entourage of the leery and unwashed. He strode up to the bike sheds, animated and angry. Even the litter, whipped up into mini-cyclones by the strengthening wind, added an extra sense of drama to the occasion.

Inky had arrived well in advance and nonchalantly leant up against the brickwork. His coat was unbuttoned to the waist, splaying out boldly at the bottom. His legs were planted firmly into the uneven ground. The Great School Detective appeared to be totally in control.

As Spud arrived, the crowd closed in behind him like the ocean behind a liner, and the pair proceeded to stare out one another.

"Think you can humiliate me, Stevens?" Spud sneered. "Think you can make up stories about me?"

"Sorry," Inky feigned, "I couldn't hear you, *Darling!*"

Barton's pal, Izzy Whizz, leaned over his shoulder, "Grab him, Spud! Do him in!"

Others took up her call:

"Kill him, Spud!"

"Smash the weirdo!"

Without breaking eye-contact, Spud began to circle Inky. "Nut allergies? Higgison's shop? Selling stuff? Peters told me all about it. Then she let me go – 'cos I'd done nothing wrong! *Nothing*, Stevens. And now I'm gonna make you pay!"

Inky eyed his adversary in cold silence. He knew that, although Spud enjoyed being the centre of attention, like all bullies he didn't really want to fight, so he was content to let Spud blow off wind knowing it was all just part of the show.

Spud wasted several more minutes posturing, jibing and swaggering before finally forcing himself to do something.

Inky knew that Spud's attack was imminent because he suddenly appeared much less sure of himself. His opening lunge, when it finally came, was forceful, but clumsy. The young detective responded like a matador. Coat flying, he simply stepped to one side and patted Spud on the head as he cannoned past and ploughed headlong into a cluster of third-years.

Spud wheeled round, his face contorted with anger, while the crowd hollered in delight, desperate for more action.

"Batter him, Spud!"

"Show him what for!"

Bristling, Spud brushed himself down, "You're gonna get it, Stevens!"

"I accept all forms of credit."

"Think you're clever, don't you?"

Grunting, Spud raised a fist, the size of a small cauliflower, and hurled it around with menace, but little control. The mob seemed uncertain. Many staggered back, wary of being struck.

Spud came at his opponent once more. This time, Inky stepped to his left, easily avoiding the attack, and before Spud could ready himself for another assault, the detective had grabbed him by the shoulder and hauled him around, gathering him up into a suffocating embrace. Spud writhed and flailed like a fish plucked from water, but Inky held on.

The crowd surged and jostled in expectation, everyone desperate for a better view.

Lightheaded, Spud lost his footing, offering Inky the opportunity to pounce. With lightning speed, the detective located a pressure point behind Spud's ear and pressed firmly. There was no pause for an intake of breath, no cry for surrender, the young thug simply fell to the floor as though he'd been shot. The crowd roared, drunk on excitement.

Inky quickly knelt to frisk his victim. Finding nothing of significance, he leaned over Spud's lifeless form and whispered into his ear, "When I click my fingers, you will awake; you will remember nothing of what has just happened, and most importantly, if it was you who took Fred Varley's keys last

Friday, you will return them to him at three o'clock today. You will knock on the Maintenance Room door and personally hand them over."

Inky then placed Spud's arm around his own neck, clicked his fingers and cried out, "I give in, Spud! I surrender!"

The crowd was dumbfounded. What had happened? How could things have changed so quickly?

Spud's eyelids flickered as he blinked back to consciousness. Seeing Inky towering over him, coupled with the crowd of onlookers all around, he immediately shot to his feet, "Urgh! Get off me, you weirdo, or I'll mash you to a pulp!"

Turning sharply, Spud caught sight of Old Hazel striding towards the bike sheds. Hazel's grape-sized wart, lit by the milky September light, seemed particularly menacing. Spud immediately let out a high-pitched scream, raised his hands skywards and ran.

The arrival of Old Hazel spelled the end of the brawl, if it could be described as that. Despite her hip complaint, the dinner-time supervisor hobbled briskly into the centre of the affray with a steely glint in her eye. She leaned up against the bike sheds, collecting her breath. "Now then, my dears, what's going on here?" she enquired, while around her hundreds of youths scattered off in all directions.

Moments later, the yard was empty except for Inky and Old

Hazel. "Was it something I said?" she asked.

****

That afternoon, Inky kept a low profile. He knew that soon Miss Peters would be demanding an explanation for the cock-and-bull story he'd concocted about Spud, but that could wait until the case of the caretaker's keys had been solved.

Just before home time, the young detective slipped away from Madam Gaudet's French class. No one saw him leave, or even noticed he'd gone. He collected his belongings from the cloakroom and trudged the empty corridors heading for Broker's Arch, situated opposite the Maintenance Room.

Broker's Arch belonged to the old part of Blinkton School, which had once formed a wing of the ancient monastery, and just to its left stood a large, oak door built directly into the crumbling stonework. A weathered sign was bolted onto it bearing the words: 'Out of Bounds!'. Ignoring this, Inky unlatched the door, pressed his shoulder against its coarse wood and barged it open.

The detective found himself in a tightly enclosed space, its air so chalky and damp that he could taste its stale grittiness. In front of him was a spiral staircase, lit by narrow slits of daylight cut into the stone walls higher up.

Inky began his ascent, one hand brushing the wall to maintain balance. He looked down as the thick slabs of stone slowly appeared, each one hollowed at the centre through centuries of use. Ahead of him, spiders scurried across pitted walls, seeking refuge. They left behind giant, gauzy webs, which dangled down like lace.

On reaching the top, Inky was confronted by a much smaller door. He collected his breath, took hold of its rusty latch and pushed it away from himself. The door caught on the ground at first, before stuttering open to reveal a rapidly darkening sky. Far off came the sound of the churning sea as it pounded the shingle of Blinkton's seashore on a never-ending loop.

As the young detective squeezed himself out through a narrow gap onto the archway itself, the cold hit him like a slap. At such a height, the fast-moving air was more savage than at ground level. Inky found himself pushing into its ferocity, face grimacing, his hair alive with movement. It was like standing on the prow of some ancient ship as it surged through Arctic waters. He fastened the top button of his coat and pressed on, moving carefully out towards the centre. There he stopped and, gripping the ancient stone wall, slowly leaned out over the school yard below. From such a height, he could see the whole of Blinkton School in miniature: building upon building, all stacked one in front of another as if competing for space. Directly beneath, he could see Fred's Maintenance Room, built onto the side of what was called the 'Old Building', and which currently acted as Mr Stanley's Statistics Office. Opposite was the Languages Department. In Room 47 he could just about make out Madam Gaudet pointing to the board.

At one minute to three, everything below was ordered and calm, but then the bell rang out and it all changed: pupils began pouring out of every possible exit; they scurried and swarmed across the playground like ants, creating patterns across the tarmac.

Amidst the throng, Inky could pick out individual students: he saw Crispin Merridew skipping happily towards Drama Club, with Ross trudging after him; he saw Rose duck out of sight behind the school minibus watching Candy Sugarcane knocking on Fred's door. Then, finally, his target appeared: Spud Barton bounded out of school with Izzy Whizz in tow, the pair of them sword fighting with plastic rulers. Spud showed no ill-effects from his lunchtime scuffle.

As Spud bundled his way past Fred's Maintenance Room door, he suddenly stopped, leaving Izzy Whizz to shoot on out alone. At the school gates, she turned to see where her pal had got to, ruler aloft, eyebrows raised. "Spud, what are you doing?" she cried.

Spud reclaimed his senses and, shaking his potato head from side to side, he turned away from Fred's room, and then, ruler aloft, he ran off towards the school gates, where his partner-in-crime was waiting.

The duo tumbled out of school and muscled their way up Wordsworth Drive. From his perch high up above, Inky Stevens had seen it all.

An icy squall troubled the detective's hair as he lifted his head towards the brooding sky. Out over the sea, a mass of angry clouds was assembling, like an invading army, and very slowly, they began to creep inland. A storm was brewing. The detective still didn't know who had stolen Fred Varley's keys, but of one thing he was certain: it wasn't Spud Barton.

CHAPTER NINE –
TO THE BAT CAVE

The mood inside Inky's room was conspiratorial; the light of the candles adding to the sense of drama.

Inky paced the floorboards deep in thought. When he spoke, his tone was direct, "Spud Barton is no longer a suspect in our case."

"How do you know that?" asked Ross.

"Trust me."

Rose laughed, "Well you certainly chose an interesting way to find out. Everyone's talking about your fight. So, who won? No one seems to know. One minute Spud was out for the count, the next he was back up again and off, wailing like a banshee."

When he spoke, Inky's voice was measured, "It wasn't about winning or losing, it was about doing what was necessary to uncover the truth, and as a result I found out that Spud didn't steal Fred's keys. But now, we need to plan for tomorrow. Time is running out, so let's hear about the other suspects."

Rose kept her voice light and purposeful, "Well, from what I've seen, Candy just drifts around in a daze. During registration, Miss Peters confiscated all her make-up and made her wipe her face clean, but after a trip to the senior girls' toilets at break time, she was painted like a circus clown again. She'd slipped out of Miss Sheldon's music lesson and managed to get hold of some slap from somewhere. Her school bag seemed to be stuffed full of it when she returned." Rose leaned forwards, consciously lowering her voice, and continued, "The strangest thing happened after school: as Candy passed Broker's Arch, she doubled back to Fred's Maintenance Room and knocked on his door. Eventually, he answered, and from what I could see, he did not look happy."

"No, he didn't," said Inky.

Rose's eyes widened, "Did you see him, too? Where were you?"

Inky's pupils appeared completely black in the half-light of the flames, "It's not important. Please go on."

"Of course," said Rose. "Yet, for all Candy's oddness, I didn't find any evidence that it was her who took Fred's keys. When Miss Peters emptied everything out of her bag, the keys weren't in there; just her usual gloop."

Ross sat up, cross-legged, "Crispin's satchel was free of keys too. I managed to search it quickly during Drama Club. I also mentioned the word 'keys' to him, but there was no reaction." His voice dropped, "Crispin seems to be quite lonely. He was in the Reflection Room all lunchtime, sitting inside the Harmony Tent on his own. I feel bad for him. He didn't speak to anyone all day, and kids make fun of him behind his back."

A silence settled over the room. Inky's pale skin reflected the dull orange of the candle flames as he weighed up everything he'd heard. Eventually, he moved over to the window and looked out into the evening, where the storm was already testing its strength.

Ross found the eerie whistling coming from outside unsettling and felt compelled to keep talking, "If nothing else," he said, "Crispin's acting in Drama Club was astonishing. He was like a person possessed. He literally *became* his father: sinister and aggressive. You should have seen Flouncy's face when he flung a table over."

"If Crispin is that good an actor, could he be hiding something?" asked Rose. "Could all this goody-two-shoes behaviour just be an act?"

"I don't think so," said Ross. "I've seen lots of odd behaviour from Crispin today, but nothing to suggest he's a thief. I quite like him in his quirky way."

Inky's voice was slow and deliberate, "Well, with Spud no longer a suspect and no evidence pointing to Candy and Crispin, Whitkirk must now become our priority. Ray Day's manner this morning has added to my general sense of unease about our Technician. Something's going on in Science."

"Day taught me in Lesson Two," said Ross, "and I found him a bit … how shall I say … *demanding*."

"Oh yes," added Rose, "Day definitely has his favourites. You're either in or out with him. And he never shuts up about cars. He goes on and on about dragsters, wheels, sprockets and whatever else gets his engine revving. It's boring."

Inky appeared to be thinking out loud, "And Day laughed when he said that Whitkirk would be back tomorrow *for sure.* He seemed to be both smug and annoyed at the same time. Plus, Whitkirk's disappearance raises questions: why was there no explanation for his absence? Where did he go? And why?"

"Yes," said Ross, folding his arms, "and what was Day doing scrabbling around in the Reflection Room?"

Inky reached into his inside pocket and produced the small device he'd discovered taped to the underside of the Reflection Room table. "I believe this is what he was so desperate to find."

Rose leaned forward for a better view, and Ross shuffled onto the end of the bed, staring at the object delicately pinched between Inky's fingers. "What is it?" he said. "It looks like something electronic."

"Some kind of radio part?" asked Rose.

Inky handed over the small, black cube, criss-crossed on its topmost surface with a series of silver, metallic lines. At opposing ends were two rows of metal prongs, sharp and symmetrical.

Ross studied it closely, "These prongs must plug into some larger machine," he said.

"And there's some writing on it," said Rose, moving in close. "There are three letters embossed on its surface: T E D."

"I think TED's an acronym," explained Inky.

"What does it stand for?"

"That, Rose," said Inky, "is what I have to find out."

The detective reached into his pocket. "Here's another thing I found at the crime scene," he said, holding up the diamond cufflink.

"Well, we can all guess who that belongs to!" said Ross.

"Making it doubly important," Inky went on, "that I intercept Whitkirk first thing tomorrow."

Inky thrust out a fist containing his final piece of evidence, "I also discovered this concealed in the flooring of the Harmony Tent. Now this is of significance." He opened his hand to reveal the brass key. Close inspection showed just how well made it was: it was robust and blocky at the lock end, yet delicately sculpted at the other, adorned with a mass of fretwork, incorporating finely-crafted swirls and detailed engravings.

"Now that's what I call a key!" said Ross.

"It's magnificent," added Rose, "like no key I've ever seen. Is that one from the missing bunch?"

"Without a doubt. It matches one of the keys Fred described to me."

Ross continued, "So what does it unlock? It looks ancient."

"That is something else I need to find out," said Inky, eyes sparkling. "Finding this key tells us one thing: whoever stole Fred's keys went into the Harmony Tent afterwards. How long afterwards, I don't know."

"So," said Rose, "when we find out who dropped that key, we solve the mystery?"

"Probably," said Inky.

Ross looked thoughtful, "According to Fred, Candy went into the tent for a lie down on Friday afternoon, and Crispin also went inside, helping to tidy up. We also know that Crispin spent all lunchtime in there today—"

Inky interrupted, "But Crispin's visit today was *after* I'd found the key."

The twins found their attention drawn back to the key being turned over and over in Inky's hand. As if reaching a decision, Inky suddenly threw it up in the air, caught hold of it and returned it to his pocket. "You've both been a great help, thank you," he said. "Tomorrow I'll need you in a more *flexible* capacity. Stay alert! Continue to monitor the movements of Crispin and Candy, and let me know immediately if you see anything of interest. We'll meet again at break time and reassess the situation. In the meantime, my priority is to find out what Whitkirk is up to and what Day is hiding. To do that I need time to plan."

Taking the hint, the twins got to their feet and began to move towards the door.

"See you tomorrow then," they said in unison.

Rose added. "And take care."

After the pair had left, Inky moved over to his bed and lay down. He laced his hands across his chest and slowly closed his eyes. Tomorrow, he realised, was going to be eventful.

CHAPTER TEN –
NOTED

The sky, which had menaced all week, chose Wednesday morning to unleash its fury: squalls of horizontal rain battered against the pebble-dashed brickwork of Blinkton's houses and gale-force winds churned up the sea beyond into a thunderous fury.

In travelling the short distance from his house to his car, Peregrine Dukes had almost been knocked off his feet by the storm, which continued to drum on the car roof throughout his journey, obliterating all other sound. No sooner had he reached the school gates than a figure came rushing towards him through the downpour and appeared at the window. He wound it open an inch, and Fred Varley thrust a soggy piece of paper through the gap. "Perry," he said, through chattering teeth, "please give this to Stevens, would you? It's urgent."

"Yes, Fred, of course, what is it?"

But Fred's response was lost to the hammering rain, and a moment later he was gone. Through his rear-view mirror, Dukes saw his friend shuffling back towards school, hunched against the deluge. His cloth cap hung askew, rainwater sliding from its peak and soaking into his overcoat. The old man looked worried; edgy. Dukes wound his window back up and looked down at what he'd been given. It was a single piece of A4 paper folded once down the middle. On the outside of the note, in spidery handwriting, were two words followed by an exclamation mark:

"Inky Stevens!"

****

Wednesday mornings meant assembly with Mr Bennett for Year Four, and Peregrine Dukes signalled that it was time for the weekly trudge to the Hall. As his form left Room 13, he discreetly steered Inky to one side to hand over Fred's note. He noted the teenager's brow furrow as he read.

"I need to be excused from assembly," said Inky, passing the note back.

Dukes nodded. Nobody would notice. "Just one less victim for Bennett's platitudes," he thought.

"I'll also need to be excused from your history class in Period

One," Inky added.

Dukes looked less sure, "Yes, yes, I suppose so, but whatever you do, don't get caught!" he said, fixing his eyes on Inky's. "If the Snake finds you, I'll deny all knowledge of your absence."

Inky nodded gravely and stepped out of Room 13 without further comment. Instead of turning left towards the Hall with the rest of his form, he turned right, heading towards one of the school's many exits.

The history teacher found himself alone in the classroom, looking down at the limp sheet of paper in his hand. He had respected Fred's privacy by not reading it up to that point, but as Inky had left it behind, he told himself that it would do no harm. With a single finger, he peeled back the top half of the paper from its crease and began to read.

"Have been in school all night. Very scared. There have been significant developments. Am in the Common Room, up in the Art Block. Perry will let you go. Must see you during registration. FV"

Dukes swallowed heavily. What were these 'developments' that had made Fred 'very scared'? He didn't mind helping his friend, but he was reluctant to be implicated in any trouble. Retirement was on the horizon, and he didn't want to leave under a cloud. He swiftly tore up the note and scattered its scraps into the waste bin. Then, with a nervous glance in either direction, he set off for the Hall to learn from Mr Bennett that 'there's a Good Samaritan inside us all'.

CHAPTER ELEVEN –
THE BREAK-IN

The Common Room was a small, carpeted room on the top floor of the Art Block. It was an intimate space where small groups of students could engage in practical activities, such as playing board games, making models or doing artwork.

Directly behind its door, there was a metal locker onto which a sign had been taped: 'Mr Beeston's Board Games Cupboard'. The locker had a dent in it at head height and its clasp hung loosely open. A discarded padlock lay on the floor beneath, accompanied bizarrely by a metal toaster which lay on its side.

Instead of chairs, the Common Room had an assortment of large, padded cubes, each with different, brightly-coloured sides – in reds, yellows and blues. It was on the yellow side of one such cube that Fred Varley sat, his overcoat still damp from the soaking he'd suffered earlier.

As Inky strode inside, Fred rose wearily, "You said I should make contact if anythin' 'appened," he said.

Inky nodded.

"Well something 'appened last night – someone broke into the school!"

"Really?" said Inky.

"I just couldn't stand the thought of leavin' the school unlocked and unprotected so I've been stayin' 'ere 'stead of goin' home. On Monday night, I slept inside the Boiler Room, and last night, I slept 'ere in the Common Room. Before I turned in, I spent me time patrollin' the school site – makin' sure everythin' was okay, see."

"And you spotted something unusual?"

"Yes," said Fred, "as I completed me fifth or sixth circuit at about nine o'clock last night, I looked up from the car park and saw summat cross in front of that window over there." He gestured towards the window. "Someone was 'ere in this room!"

"Who?"

"Whoever it was who stole me keys. It was dark so I only caught a glimpse, but there was someone in 'ere. Then, I noticed that the door to the Art Block was open, which was strange 'cos I knew Miss Trout would have locked it with her own keys when she left at about four."

"What did you do?" asked Inky.

"I tried to sort it out meself, didn't I? I couldn't call no one; there's only me, you and Perry knows about them missing keys, so I crept up the stairs and made me way to the other side of that door, there. I peered in through the glass, but couldn't see nothin'. Thought I must have 'magined it, so I opened the door and tiptoed in."

"And what happened?"

"All hell broke loose, that's what bloomin' 'appened!"

Inky remained silent.

"Someone were waitin' for me, weren't they?" The caretaker pointed at the games cupboard. "Whoever it were, were hiding behind that locker, and as I sneaked in, they leapt out and hit me over the 'ed from behind with that." Fred pointed to the toaster. "Fair shook me up it did, Master Stevens, I can tell you. I saw stars."

Inky tilted his head and sucked in his cheeks with concern. "Are you alright?"

"Yes, yes, I'm fine. Good job I 'ad me cap on. Protected me from the worst of it. Got a bloomin' lump on me forehead, though." He raised his hat to reveal a swelling the size of a marble.

"I wanted to let you know about it as soon as possible so that you could check out the scene of the crime – for clues an' that."

"You did a risky thing," said Inky, scrutinising the room. "The person who broke in last night must have done so for a reason. Is there anything missing?"

"Dunno. Thought I'd leave the detectin' to you. But I have discovered summat." He rose with a grunt and shuffled back over to the locker. "The games cupboard is usually locked with that padlock there on the floor. There's only two keys to it: Mr Beeston's and the one on me missing bunch."

Inky's face was a mask of concentration. "Did you see who attacked you?" he asked.

"No, it was over too quickly. I just crept in 'ere, and before I knew it, wallop! I was on the ground. Whoever it were who clobbered me scarpered sharpish."

"You didn't see anything?"

"I saw the back of 'im. When I came to, I looked out of the window and saw a dark shadow tearin' off. He jumped over that wall at the far end of the car park and disappeared with summat under 'is arm."

"The intruder took something?"

Fred looked across as if the thought had never occurred to him, "I think so."

"Well," said Inky, "let's find out."

The young detective kicked the padlock aside and approached the locker. He tugged gently at its handle, and at once, a mass of games paraphernalia came tumbling out: cards, tokens, dice, paper money, plastic counters, a metal top hat, two white chess kings and two black queens, a mini pickaxe, several marbles and a miniature terrier figurine.

Inky studied the mess strewn across the carpet. Satisfied that there was nothing suspicious among the debris, he turned his attention to the cupboard.

"What's been taken?" asked Fred.

"We can easily find out," said Inky, pointing towards the handwritten list taped onto the inside of the locker door. "Here's Mr Beeston's inventory: *Buckaroo (3), Twister (2), Monopoly (4), Chess (2), Mousetrap (1), Kerplunk (3)* etcetera. And look at these shelves; there are labels to indicate where everything should go. Are you up for a challenge?"

"I guess," replied Fred reluctantly.

"Good. I need you to sort out this mess. Put all these items back into their correct boxes and put each box onto its correct shelf. Then you need to cross-reference all the items against the inventory. That will tell us whether anything is missing or, to be more exact, what it was that the culprit was after."

Fred's eyes slid across the room, from the mess on the floor, up to the locker, down to the toaster and then back to Inky. "May I ask what you've learned so far, Master Stevens, about the case? Are you close to findin' out who took me keys?"

Inky raised a hand, "Be patient. There's no time to explain, but I will soon, I promise. Right now, I need to speak to Mr Whitkirk, but before I go, I'd like to ask a couple of questions."

"Fire away," said Fred.

Inky continued, "You described your attacker as a 'he'."

"Did I?" Fred thought for a moment. "I couldn't see much," he said, "but I'd say that the figure I saw in the car park were male rather than female; and not too tall neither."

"More like a student than an adult?"

"Yes, now I think about it, but I can't be one hundred per cent sure."

Inky took a second to process this new information.

"And finally," said Inky, "Do you recognise this?"

Fred gasped as Inky fished in his pocket and produced a small key.

"Of course," said Fred, his eyes lighting up. "It's the key I told you about – the key to Blinkton's vault. Now that key were *definitely* on me bunch. Where did you find it?"

"And this vault contains?" asked Inky, ignoring Fred's question.

"All Blinkton School's information: exam results, student files, photographs, newspaper clippings, every-bloomin'-thing."

Although Inky's expression remained blank, a light bulb had

suddenly switched on inside his head. On and off it flashed without missing a beat – bright red in colour. Inky forced himself to focus on what Fred was saying.

"Anythin' of any importance whatsoever is inside Mr Stanley's vault," Fred continued. "If you have access to that room, you have access to the whole school archive."

Inky pushed on, "How many keys are there to this vault?"

"Two. Mr Stanley has one and I 'ave – I mean I 'ad – the other; the one you 'ave there."

Inky slipped it back into his pocket, "Thank you, Fred, you've been most helpful. Now, I'll leave you to find out what's been taken from Mr Beeston's cupboard, if anything. If you do spot something missing, please write it down on a piece of paper and ask Miss Cartwright to pass it to me in Lesson Two. I have maths in Room 14 with Miss Spiller."

Fred nodded, then without another word, the detective spun around, flung the door open and disappeared, sweeping off to science with added determination.

CHAPTER TWELVE –
THE WORSENING DAY

Inky made it to the Science Office just ahead of the nine o'clock bell. As soon it started to *trill*, the door whipped open and Ray Day burst out, exactly as he had done the day before.

Day stopped abruptly, "Nearly ran you over there, Ink-o!" he boomed. "I'm late, so make it quick! What can I do you for, Amigo?"

Inky repeated the same message as the previous day.

Day stared at the young detective, his eyes darkening, "Science project for Whitt-o, eh? I'd forget that for now if I were you."

"But, I spoke to you yesterday, Sir," Inky persisted. "You told me that Mr Whitkirk was absent and that I should come back tomorrow, which is now today, so here I am."

Day's large forehead wrinkled like folds in fabric. "Look,

Stevens, things have happened over the past couple of days – unpleasant things – so I wouldn't trouble Mr Whitkirk. Whatever you want will have to wait."

Inky refused to be deterred, "With all due respect, Sir, it won't. I need to finish my physics assignment for this afternoon, so it's important that I see Mr Whitkirk now because he said he'd help. And yesterday you said that—"

Day prickled, "Look, Ink-o, I don't have time for this. You have a little science project going on – great! You want Whitt-o to help you with it – bully for you! But, he's not available, so just do me a favour and give that creepy little head of yours a rest. Make like a banana and split!"

Day side-stepped Inky, and as he moved off, the reflection from the strip lights drew uneven lines across his polished skull. Inky allowed Ray Day the luxury of exactly four strides before calling out after him, "Don't worry, Mr Day, there are plenty other things to get revved up about, such as the TED."

Day paused for a beat, then wheeled round and came careering after Inky like a bowling ball, "Stop right there, Stevens!" he yelled, grabbing the detective by the collar and then pushing him back against the wall by his lapels. "What did you say?"

But Inky refused to be intimidated. "Assaulting a minor won't look good on your CV, or in the *Blinkton Gazette*, or on the national news."

Day's grip tightened, "Tell me what you know about the TED."

"I'd prefer it if you told me where I can find Mr Whitkirk first."

At that moment, a cluster of first-year girls appeared around the corner. They took one look at the scene and retreated in fright.

Day's face froze, until finally he managed to regain a sense of perspective. He looked about himself uncertainly and released his grip, smoothing down the leather of Inky's coat with the back of his shovel-hands. Initially, he tried to look apologetic, but falling some distance short, the science teacher stepped back and raised his hands instead, "Come on, Ink-o, let's not overreact. How about I tell you where Whitt-o is, and then you can tell me about the TED?"

Inky folded his arms, "I'm listening."

"Okay," Day sighed, "at this moment, Whitt-o is inside the Snake's Office, but if you want to see him, you'd better get up there pronto; I have a feeling he's not going to be around for much longer."

Inky hid his surprise. "There, that wasn't hard, was it?" he said and turned swiftly to leave, only to find himself wheeled back around under the weight of a heavy paw.

"You seem to be forgetting something, Ink-o; what about the TED?"

Inky wriggled free, "The TED is safe. *If* everything works out nicely, I'll be more than happy to return it to its rightful owner. Don't leave town, Day-o! I'll be in touch."

Day watched the black-coated teenager head off in the direction of the Snake's Office. "This isn't finished, Stevens," he swore to himself. "Make a fool of me and there'll be a price to pay!"

****

Blinkton School's Reception was the Snake's pride and joy. The entire space was gleaming white and as fresh as an Icelandic glacier. Directed lighting bounced off polished chrome, and a vase of lilies sat on top of a welcome desk, which was angled to face the entrance doors. Tucked away behind this, almost obscured from view, was a door that led into the Snake's Office – a mini-fortress, complete with bulletproof, mirrored window.

Receptionist Ginny Cartwright sat behind the welcome desk, sporting a smile that displayed every penny of her expensive dental work. Once a runner-up in the Miss Blinkton Beauty Pageant, she possessed all the credentials the Snake deemed essential for her to be 'the face of Blinkton': her auburn hair hung free with natural bounce; her make-up was tasteful; and her demeanour was business-like, cheery and efficient.

It was towards Miss Cartwright's desk that the Great School Detective made his way with a degree of haste. As he neared the Reception, his pace slowed and then stopped altogether, as he concealed himself a short distance away inside an alcove. Within seconds, he could hear Whitkirk's clipped voice drifting across the pristine space from the direction of the Snake's Office.

The investigator strained to make out what was being said, his hearing impeded by the thickness of the office door. For Inky, the snatches of conversation he caught were almost worse than hearing nothing at all. Words passed into his consciousness, but he could barely make sense of them: 'resignation', 'two-faced', 'Mr Day', 'can't stand any more'. His task was further hindered by a succession of telephone calls bombarding the school switchboard:

"What's that, Miss Hassell?" said Miss Cartwright, her voice like honey. "Hetty Brimscoll's lost her locker key in the pool changing rooms?"

"Mrs Morris, you need the petty cash box unlocked?"

"Sorry, Mr Foreshaw, what did you say? You think you saw a student on top of Broker's Arch yesterday afternoon? The door to the spiral staircase may be unlocked?"

And in every case, the Receptionist's reply was the same: "I'll log your concern and ask Fred to come right away with his keys."

It seemed the results of Fred's missing keys were beginning to reverberate throughout the school, but before Inky could reflect on the problem, Whitkirk suddenly appeared, bursting out of the Snake's Office, ruddy-cheeked and frowning. He tore through the Reception like a tornado, past Miss Cartwright's desk and then past Inky's hiding place. The young detective didn't think twice; he was off and after him, with the Receptionist's startled voice following him down the corridor, "Inky Stevens, what on earth are you doing here?"

****

Wilfred Whitkirk flew through school at double-speed, his lab coat flying out wildly behind him, hair bobbing and moustache quivering. He rocketed along the Performing Arts corridor until he neared his destination. On reaching the Reflection Room, he paused briefly to peer in, then burst inside.

Inky watched him disappear from a safe distance, then tip-toed up to the door and looked inside. There, bathed in red and orange light, Blinkton's Science Technician was lying on his back, clawing at the underside of the table, unaware that the object he sought was inside Inky's desk drawer at home. He stood up in dismay, running a hand through his immaculate hair, before turning abruptly and storming back out.

Wary of being spotted, Inky took a sudden interest in a display board. Whitkirk thundered past him again, rounded a corner and bounded up the staircase towards the Science Department. Once there, he unlocked the Office door and stormed inside.

The Science Office was small, cluttered and permanently smelled of sulphur. It acted as a hub at the heart of the Science Department from which several doors led off into different laboratories. All the available wall space was decorated with an assortment of science posters: the solar system, the periodic table, the workings of the combustion engine. There was a life-size plastic skeleton in the far corner, suspended on a metal pole. This had been dressed by the Department in a school blazer and tie, and a nameplate hung around its neck proclaiming: 'Napoleon Bone-Apart'.

When Inky entered, Whitkirk was standing with his back to him, bundling an assortment of items into a carrier bag. He wheeled around sharply, looking resplendent in his spotless lab coat, steam-pressed trousers and spotted bow tie. A frown immediately settled across his face, "Stevens? What are you doing here? Why aren't you in class?"

"Sorry to disturb you, Sir, but I need your help."

Without giving Whitkirk time to object, Inky removed an object from his rucksack and thrust it towards him. "I think this belongs to you, Sir," he said, holding it up towards the light.

Whitkirk's mouth fell open, and he automatically held out a hand. "Thank you, Stevens, I thought I'd lost that for good," he said. "Where did you find it?"

"Inside the Reflection Room. I believe you lost it last Friday during Lesson Five."

Whitkirk ran a hand through his hair, which immediately sprang back into place. "How do you know where I was on Friday?"

"I had a meeting with Mr Day this morning," said Inky, tossing the cufflink towards him.

Whitkirk snatched it, then looked across at the young detective uncertainly. "It must have come loose when I went to collect Mr Day's record," he said.

"Or when you were doing something else, perhaps?"

Whitkirk looked hard at Inky.

"You don't like Fred Varley, do you, Sir?" said Inky.

Whitkirk frowned, "I beg your pardon?"

"You don't, though, do you?" Inky persisted.

"I don't think about him much. What has this got to do with you?"

"You embarrassed Fred in front of the governors before an important meeting, and there's been hostility between the two of you ever since."

"Did I? Has there?" Whitkirk seemed taken aback. "Oh yes, I remember; I plugged the coffee machine in for him, if that's what you mean?"

Inky continued, "Not especially fond of Ray Day, are you, Sir?"

Traces of anger bubbled up though Whitkirk's usual calmness, "What is this, Stevens? What are you driving at? I've just about had enough of you and Ray Day and the whole of Blinkton School."

"I'd like you to talk to me about the TED," said Inky calmly.

Whitkirk's eyes widened in surprise, "The TED? Have you got it?"

"It's safe," continued Inky, "But what is it for, and why is it so important to you and Mr Day?"

Outside, the ten o'clock bell could be heard signalling the start of Lesson Two. Whitkirk let out a long sigh, "Very well, Stevens, tell me what you know about the TED, and I'll fill in the blanks. I've nothing to lose."

Inky leaned back against a workbench and recounted some of what he knew: "Last Friday you entered the Reflection Room carrying a clipboard and a roll of tape on an errand for Mr Day. Fred Varley was changing the electric sockets in there at the time. Whilst collecting some record or other, you taped a small electronic device under the table at the far side of the room. The cufflink I've just given to you came loose and lodged behind the table leg." He went on, "The device is now in my possession. It has the letters T E D inscribed across its surface. What do they stand for?"

Whitkirk brushed an imaginary piece of lint from his sleeve, "T E D stands for 'transponder electrification device.'"

"Some kind of motor engine part?"

"How did you know?"

"Well if it's important to Mr Day, it must have something to do with racing."

Whitkirk allowed himself a faint smile, "I'm impressed, Stevens. It's the TED that improves the performance of Day's dragster. It fastens into a groove on the top of the engine. When the lights turn green, it redirects a huge energy surge from the engine capacitor onto his back axle, and this in turn … Let's just say that it makes his dragster go faster; much faster."

"And Mr Day wins the race?"

The Technician nodded, "Yeah, I do all the brain-bending, while he takes all the applause and the prize money too."

Whitkirk ran a finger along the bench top, "But winning one race isn't enough for him; Day needs to win *every* race. He yearns for that buzz, time after time."

"And to achieve that, he needs you."

Whitty rolled his eyes and nodded, "But I don't want to be Ray Day's understudy. In fact, I don't want anything to do with him at all. Helping big bullies win car races is not what I spent three years at university for."

"Well can't Mr Day do it himself? He is Head of Science after all."

Whitkirk laughed, "School science is easy, but drag racing is different. In drag racing being good is not good enough. To be successful you need to be exceptional. And on his own, Ray Day is *not* exceptional."

"So, your argument with the Snake was about Mr Day, not Fred Varley?"

Whitkirk looked puzzled, "Sorry, Stevens, I don't know what all this business with Fred is about. Honestly, I don't. Last Friday, I'd reached breaking point, and picking up that record for Day was just one meaningless errand too far."

"And at that point, you decided it was time to teach him a lesson by removing the TED and hiding it."

Whitkirk nodded, "But taking away his precious toy only made things worse. He didn't win his big race at the weekend, so when I came into work on Monday, he started to take it out on me. At that point, I decided enough was enough; I told him where the TED was hidden and went home."

"Hence you weren't in school yesterday."

"Hence I wasn't in school yesterday."

"But Mr Day said he knew you'd be back today for sure. Was that because the Snake summoned you?"

"Yes, she called me in to account for myself, and I thought that if I could explain about the TED to her, she might be reasonable, but as things turned out, our esteemed Headmistress didn't want to hear. Day had got to her first and poisoned her mind against me. I realised then that it was the end for me."

Inky tried to steer the discussion back towards to his investigation, "So it was Day's resignation you were calling for, not Fred's?"

Whitkirk looked confused, "This has nothing to do with Fred at all, and I'd never ask the Snake to sack anyone, not even Ray Day. I just wanted things to change, that's all. No, it was me who resigned."

Inky took a moment to take this in, "And the Snake accepted?"

"In a blink. She gave me half an hour to collect my things and get out. So, much as I've enjoyed this little cross-examination, the goings on in this school are no longer my concern."

Inky watched Whitkirk shuffle towards the door, head bent over, "Don't you want to know where the TED is, Sir?"

"Keep it. Just don't let Day have it! Let him suffer. He's run me out of town, but he'll come off worse in the long run." The Technician placed a hand on the door handle, but before he could turn it, the door immediately crashed in on him – the result of a stout blow from a thick-soled boot – and Ray Day's hulking figure reared up like a colossus in the doorway.

CHAPTER THIRTEEN –
A FRIEND INDEED

That Wednesday, Perry Dukes covered for Inky as promised. At the start of Lesson One, he simply placed an 'X' instead of an 'O' against Inky's name in the register, and then he headed down to the Maintenance Room to check on the young detective's progress.

"I sent Inky to meet you in registration. I let him off history too. Was he any use?" Dukes asked his caretaker friend.

Fred ignored the question. "I'm beaten, Perry," he said mournfully, "I'll never work again. Not here, not anywhere. It was stupid of me – stupid, stupid, stupid."

Perry attempted to lighten the mood, "Nonsense, Fred, old chap! These things wash over; they always do. Think of history: terrible things have happened in the past, but humanity soldiers on."

"Perry?"

"Yes?"

"Shut up, would you? It's over, don't you see? Poor Hetty Brimscoll lost her locker key during swimming, and as far as I know, she's still in her swimsuit. Mrs Morris has made some complaint or other and there's loads others of flooding in. Me phone has hardly stopped ringin'; I've taken it off the hook. I feel as though there's a noose around me neck and it's gettin' tighter. Last night, someone broke into the games cupboard in the Art Block and stole—'

"Someone broke in? Why?"

"It doesn't matter, nothing does any more. Tomorrow at nine o'clock, I'll be in the Snake's Office receivin' me bloomin' marchin' orders."

"Don't despair," said Dukes. "What does Inky say?"

Fred was dismissive, "Inky? He's doin' his best. He says progress has been made, but I just don't think that—"

"Well then," said Dukes, lifting his voice, "that sounds positive! Inky usually sorts things out. Just give him time."

Fred wiped his beard, "But that's just it; we don't 'ave time, and Stevens is just a schoolkid. I appreciate 'is efforts an' all, but he is never goin' to get them keys back before nine o'clock tomorrow, is he? Unless—"

Dukes jumped on Fred's final word, "Unless what?" he

asked, wide-eyed.

"Nothin'. I'm just graspin' at bloomin' straws."

Dukes persisted, "Come on, tell me, what's on your mind?"

"Well," he said, "you know this meetin' with the Snake at nine o'clock tomorrow. Now, I can't be late, but I don't have to *open* her safe at nine. I could delay her, say by talking about the swimming pool, or lack of car park lightin', or … no, it won't work. It still won't give us enough time."

But Dukes refused to be put off, "Look, Fred, every bit of extra time could be vital. Knowing Inky, he'll probably turn up at the Snake's Office and save you in the nick of time, like in those silly detective stories."

Fred shifted, "Well, I might be able to delay the Snake for about thirty minutes, perhaps thirty-five at a push, but I'm not sure it'll make any difference. I'm being daft, but if by any miracle Inky has found me keys, tell 'im to come straight into the Snake's Office as soon as registration ends, even if he has to return 'em right in front of her. I'll deal with the consequences."

"You shouldn't have to deal with anything; you're the one who's been wronged. What is important is that whoever stole your keys is brought to task. It's the thief who ought to be worried; not you."

Dukes pushed himself up using the arms of Fred's chair, "Look, I'm sorry, but I have to go, or else I'll be late for class."

Fred blew his nose, then made to stand.

"No, that's okay, Fred. Take your time. Finish your tea and biscuit. I'll pass on your message."

Fred forced a smile. "Thanks, Perry, you're a true friend."

CHAPTER FOURTEEN –
OFF IN A CLOUD OF SMOKE

Ray Day filled the doorway of the Science Office trapping both Inky and Whitkirk inside. He slammed the door shut and brought his fist down hard onto a work surface. Chemical bottles scattered and the air filled with a stench of chlorine so thick that it burned the back of Inky's throat. Day pushed Whitkirk aside and cannoned on towards Napoleon Bone-Apart, causing a tray of litmus paper to fall from a high shelf and send a ticker-tape parade fluttering down. A canister of dry ice also tumbled, and a layer of dense, white smoke spread out over the floor, like a living carpet.

Having reached the skeleton, Day grabbed hold of its femur. As he yanked the thigh bone free from its pelvis, a sickly sucking sound rang out. He then raised the femur over his head and advanced towards Inky.

"Like a bad penny, you keep turning up, don't you, Stevens? This time, you're in for it."

Inky stood up straight. "I'm not in for it," he snapped, "because if you bash my brains out with a plastic leg, you'll never see the TED again."

At the mention of the motor engine component, Day's eyes immediately shrank. He looked at Whitkirk, "This is your fault, Whitt-o," he snarled, prodding him with his makeshift club.

Inky was quick to respond, "To use a biological metaphor, Day-o, I wouldn't vent your spleen on Mr Whitkirk. He's endured enough of your bullying."

Reluctantly, Day let his weapon drop to the ground, where it disappeared into the swirling mass of fog.

"Go on then, Whitt-o!" Day snarled. "Scram! You can leave, but only because your guardian angel here seems intent on blackmailing me."

Whitkirk crouched down and began to scrabble about for his belongings. Groping frantically, he located his carrier bag and staggered towards the door with it tucked under his arm.

"Not so fast, Whitt-o," said Day. "Take that cheap bag of junk by all means, but I want your lab coat – it's school property – and I want the keys to my classrooms too."

With trembling hands, the Technician reached into his

pocket and produced a small bunch of keys. He slung them across a workbench until they came to rest against a life-sized plastic head used to demonstrate the mechanics of the brain. Next, he removed his lab coat and flung it to the floor – the dry ice curling upwards in response. Without his coat, Wilfred Whitkirk looked vulnerable, his runner-bean frame containing only marginally more flesh than Bone-Apart's. Standing there with bright red braces exposed against a crisp, white shirt only added to his awkwardness.

Whitkirk gave Day a look of disdain and then sped out into the corridor. He left without looking back, his carrier bag slapping against his leg and wisps of dry ice clinging to his heels.

Inky found himself alone with the science teacher. "Feel proud of yourself, Day-o?" he said. "Picking on someone a quarter your weight and four times your intelligence?"

Day cradled giant hands behind his basketball head, "You'd better leave, too, Stevens," he leered. "I want the TED back, and you're going to fetch it for me. You *will* return what is mine. Now go quickly. Because," he spewed out a volcano of rage, "ripping your arms from their sockets and beating you about the head with them is the only thing that could improve my mood this morning!"

The detective hitched his rucksack onto his back and made

to leave, "Your morning is going to get far worse," he said calmly. "Every action has an equal and opposite reaction. You ought to know that."

Inky set off in the same direction as Whitkirk, albeit at a more sedate pace. As he headed towards maths, a distinctive sound rolled out down the corridor after him – that of a plastic cranium connecting with the back of the Science Office door.

****

Mathematics had taken on a whole new importance at Blinkton School. The Snake desperately wanted to get her talons on the inter-school PJ Ward Prize for Mathematics, and nothing would deflect her from this aim. Of course, this had put undue pressure on the Maths Department – pressure which had been passed down via the Head of Mathematics Marjorie Spiller ('Killer Spiller') to the students themselves.

That Wednesday morning, Spiller patrolled the maths class silently, wearing flat, black shoes, tan-coloured tights, a tweed skirt and a beige cardigan wrapped tightly around her sinewy frame. She had already established a mood of hushed discipline and was not about to tolerate any disturbance.

When Inky arrived fifteen minutes late for her lesson following his confrontation with Day, the whole room took a sharp intake of breath. Not one student dared to looked up, engaged as they were in a series of tasks to determine the values of x, y and z according to a succession of varying conditions.

Killer was furious; she squinted at Inky with eyes screwed so far back into her head they looked like little black buttons. "Sit down, Stevens!" she demanded in her thin and cheerless voice. "We're on page 37. Make sure you catch up!"

Inky took his seat beside the window, opened his maths book and immediately began to grapple with a series of equations. However, his concentration was soon broken by a gentle knock on the door, followed by the arrival of the glamorous Receptionist.

"Excuse me, Miss Spiller," said Miss Cartwright, avoiding the maths teacher's Medusa stare, "I have a message for Inky Stevens."

"Stevens indeed? He seems intent on disrupting everyone's advancement today. Very well, but be quick!"

Miss Cartwright threaded her way towards Inky's desk and handed over a single piece of paper, "Fred sent this for you. He said you'd be expecting it. Poor fellah has an awful bump on his head; do you know anything about it?"

"Miss Cartwright!" snapped Killer from the front, "I believe the remit of your errand has expired!"

"Yes, Miss Spiller," she replied quickly and left the room feeling a little like a schoolchild herself.

Before the door had closed, Inky had transferred Fred's

note to his knee, where he smoothed it out and read its brief contents:

"One complete chess set is missing from the Common Room. FV"

For the remainder of the lesson, part of Inky's mind grappled with the correlation of a meaningless set of numbers and letters, while another part shuffled through the facts of his case: "Who would break into school late at night and risk everything just to steal a chess set?" he asked himself.

The heavy silence inside Room 14 helped Inky to focus; and through the whirling fog of his thoughts, a solution gradually began to take shape …

CHAPTER FIFTEEN – BACKSTAGE ACTIVITY

During morning break, Inky Stevens was sitting in the doorway of his makeshift office behind the school stage, as planned. In his hand, he held the ornate key he'd found in the Reflection Room. He turned this over and over between his fingers, as though manipulating rosary beads. The case of the caretaker's keys was proving to be far from straightforward, but although he lacked proof, he finally knew who the culprit was.

Before he could think further, he was interrupted by two sets of footsteps struggling to negotiate the backstage blackness. The Berrys arrived in a state of excitement and immediately bombarded Inky with questions:

"Why weren't you at assembly?"

"There are rumours about a disturbance in the Science Office. Was that anything to do with you?"

"Do you know that Whitty has left the school?"

"Enough!" said Inky, "Time is scarce and there's a lot to do. I think I've established who took Fred's keys, but I need to find out why."

"Who was it?" asked Ross.

"I can't let you know just yet; there are too many loose ends," said Inky, "and I need evidence to support my theory, but I know what I must do next, thanks to this little thing here." He held the ornate key aloft. "If we're successful, then our case will be solved before sunrise."

"Have you worked out what it opens, Inky?" said Rose

"It's the key to the vault inside Mr Stanley's office."

"The Statistics Office?" said Ross. "I've never seen anyone go inside there other than Wiggy himself."

Inky's eyes shone through the dark, "Yes, he's very protective of his office, which makes the next part of our mission difficult. But no investigation is without risk, and the evidence we need to solve the case is locked in there, so I'll need you to help me get inside."

There was a brief pause. Rose looked at Ross, Ross looked at Rose, then two heads pivoted back towards Inky, "You want us to help you enter the vault?" they said.

But the detective was already on the move, striding off towards the main body of the school. He navigated through the backstage gloom with the twins clambering after him. Inky called out over his shoulder, "It's crucial we make no mistakes. Rose, please continue to watch Candy. I also need you to check the contents of Miss Peters' desk drawer."

"How?"

"Find a way," he said dryly.

The young detective parted the stage curtains, continued down a small flight of wooden steps and then strode out into the hall, "Ross, keep watch on Crispin as before, but whatever you do, do not be seen or make contact with him!"

"Yes."

"I won't be attending lessons for the rest of the day, so Rose, I'll need you to explain to Miss Pinkerton why I'm missing in Lesson Four; and Ross, I need you to do likewise with Chalky for Lesson Five; say whatever you like, be inventive, just make it believable."

"What about PE?" said Ross.

Inky called out, "Everyone knows that PE's not a proper subject. Spencer won't notice whether I'm there or not."

On reaching the Hall doors, Inky halted so abruptly that the twins nearly ran into the back of him, "I'd like you to report back to me after school, right on the bell, beneath Broker's Arch. Okay?"

"Understood," they said.

Inky was on the move once more, threading along the school's rabbit warren of corridors, past an army of schoolchildren who had opted to stay inside out of the storm. As he rounded the corner of the Performing Arts Department, he came face to face with the one person he was keen to avoid.

"Ah, Stevens!" came the cry. "A private word, if you'd be so good?"

Miss Peters was standing beside the statue of Lionel Roebuck on break duty ...

CHAPTER SIXTEEN –
THE VAULT

Maxwell ('Wiggy') Stanley was in his sixties and had only lasted in education so long because he didn't have to teach. Being Blinkton's Statistics Officer gave him a senior position without requiring him to go anywhere near a classroom. He'd earned his nickname from the ridiculous hairpiece he wore – a dense frisbee of bright, ginger hair, which sat on top of his head and couldn't even be relied on to face the right direction.

The Statistics Office was located opposite the Broker's Arch staircase, next door to Fred's Maintenance Room. As part of the old monastery, it retained some of its medieval character. Built from thick stone, it was spartan and grim, with a single window located high up, arched in shape and protected by iron bars. A desk and chair were positioned centrally on a crimson rug – the room's only splash of colour. However, the office's most striking feature was a heavy, iron door, set into the wall just to the left of the entrance. The side of the door facing into the office comprised a single sheet of dull, slate-grey metal, its plane broken by a series of studs around the edges, a brass handle, and a keyhole set into its centre. As a portal, it was impressive-looking, giving an overall sense of gravitas to the function it performed: guarding Blinkton School's most important documents.

Inside the enormous room beyond the door, Stanley catalogued and stored the school's archives. The vault was his private sanctuary, where he could collate all the school's data in peace, tucked away from rampaging school children. But on this Wednesday, his peace was about to be disturbed. As the Statistician sat at his desk ordering the stock for next week's school dinners, there came a distinctive knock on the door.

Outside, Inky pulled up his collar against the driving rain and waited patiently before trying a second time. Ross hovered at his shoulder, already soaked, "What are you going to say when Wiggy opens up?"

"Nothing."

"Nothing?"

"Yes, because *you're* going to do the talking."

And as the handle began to turn, Inky stepped aside and nudged Ross forwards.

Stanley opened the door a fraction and peered out. All that was visible was one bespectacled eye, "Yes?" he croaked.

Ross was startled by how large Stanley's eye appeared through his spectacles – all bloodshot and blinking, "Erm …" he said.

"What is it?" snapped Stanley.

"Erm … We're conducting a geography survey for Miss Entwistle, and we need as many respondents as possible."

"What? I'm sorry, but I'm very busy—"

"It would only take a couple of minutes," Rose added.

"Try the Staff Room. I'm sure someone there will help you," said Stanley's eye. "I'm tied up right now."

"How often do you visit the Funshine Arcade?" said Rose in an official voice.

"I beg your pardon?"

Rose repeated, "The Funshine Arcade on the seafront. How often would you say that you visit? Every day, every week, every month or once a year? Or none of the above?"

"And," she continued, "on the way home, are you likely to indulge in a portion of fish and chips from The Codfather, or pizza from Don Marco's or kebabs from Speedy's or a Mexican from Tequila Mockingbird? Or all of the above?"

"None of the above," said Stanley, "I'm sorry, but I really don't have time—"

"We have to collect data," said Ross, sliding his foot into the crack in the door.

"Yes," Rose pleaded, "we need to acquire accurate statistical information about Blinkton-on-Sea, then analyse it and produce a graph, pie-chart or bar-chart."

"Or even a scatter-diagram!" Ross added.

"So," said Rose, taking out an exercise book and sliding a pen into the corner of her mouth, "would you mind awfully spending a couple of minutes providing us with some data?"

Rose could sense rather than see Stanley thawing at the mention of his favourite word. After a brief pause, his office door opened and he stepped out. "Why didn't you say so?" he exclaimed. "Statistics are my domain, my *raison d'etre*. There's nothing about data collection I don't know. I'll tell you what, I'll provide you with all the information you need, and then we can discuss the best way for you to present it."

Stanley was immediately submerged in a world in which he felt comfortable, and having been taken in, he was easily prompted to answer all kinds of meaningless questions. Hairpiece shaking, he gestured passionately, oblivious to the rain sliding down his plastic follicles and soaking his gown.

Meanwhile, Inky slipped unnoticed behind the animated Statistician and into the sombre coolness of the Statistics Office beyond.

****

Wiping a bead of rainwater from his eye, Inky stood in front of the vault door a few paces inside the Statistics Office and inserted the ornate key he'd found into the keyhole at its centre. Using his free hand to muffle any sound, he turned it cautiously, feeling its mechanism yield with a faint click. The young detective exhaled before turning his attention to the handle. He gently pulled down the shiny, brass lever, again cushioning it to prevent unwanted noise.

There was another series of short, muffled clunks before the great iron slab finally surrendered. Despite its size, the door swung outwards easily, and from the blackness beyond, a whisper of stale air oozed out – the suffocating aroma of decades of education.

Inky reached for the light switch set into the wall to the left of the vault door. With a click, several banks of lights immediately pinked into life, bathing the vault in a wash of muted fluorescence. The space was cavernous: a vast library of information; row upon row of identical shelves reached outwards from a central aisle to both the right and left and extended to the ceiling. Placed onto these were hundreds of wooden crates, all brimming with folders – identical, save for the labelling. And every folder, in turn, was stuffed full of documents.

There were hundreds of thousands of individually catalogued pieces of paper contained in the vault; every document that had ever been issued by Blinkton School: documents relating to teachers and ancillary employees, building plans and developments, finances, examinations, photographs, prospectuses, sick notes – absolutely everything. And every crate had been arranged chronologically, with the oldest ones deep within the recesses of the vault.

Every academic year had its own shelf, every year group its own crate, and every student had his or her own alphabetically arranged file. The entire undertaking had been compiled and catalogued solely by Maxwell Stanley. Everything had its rightful place and, thanks to Stanley's meticulous indexing, everything could be found with the minimum of fuss.

****

At twenty-past eleven the school bell rang, and Stanley immediately snapped out of his trance. He broke off mid-sentence, pulled his gown about him, and dismissed the twins. "I hope that I have been of help," he said. "Perhaps we can continue this some other time? Now, if you'll excuse me, I have important work to attend to, and you must go to your lessons."

As he disappeared abruptly behind his door, a multitude of raindrops *plopped* down from its frame onto the tarmac below.

This was followed immediately by the sound of a key turning in the lock and a pained grunt.

"Well," said Rose, "we've done what Inky asked us to do; we got him inside. Let's just hope that he can get out again."

"Inky knows what he's doing," said Ross, and then decided to lighten the mood, "Who would have thought, Rose, that Wiggy's favourite kitchen utensil would be sugar tongs?"

****

Grunting in irritation, Maxwell Stanley removed his gown and jacket, then flopped down onto his chair to resume his calculations for next week's menu.

Inside the vault, Inky realised that he had only a short time left in which to operate. He set about his task with purpose, working briskly and methodically. First, he approached the shelving unit to his left, carefully tracing the words written on each box with a finger, then he counted two crates along and four up to locate the one labelled 'Second Year'. Reaching above his head, Inky found his first piece of evidence with ease. In fact, the file he was after had not even been stored away inside its crate; it was sitting on top instead. Catching Inky by surprise, it tumbled downwards as he reached for it, its contents scattering.

Inky bent to retrieve the documents, not wishing to leave behind any trace of his presence. Reassured, he leaned against a set of stepladders, neatly placed the stack of papers on his knee and began to sort through them.

The Great School Detective never relied on luck. He believed that results were attained through logic and dogged determination. Occasionally a twist of fate worked in his favour, but occasionally events seemed to go against him, and so it was to prove at that moment. He had barely finished studying Crispin Merridew's file when the vault lights went out and blackness engulfed him.

CHAPTER SEVENTEEN –
HERE, THERE AND EVERYWHERE

It wasn't until lunchtime that Rose set about the task Inky had given her. She made her way to Miss Peters' Office wondering what it was that Inky expected her to find in the Head of Year's drawer and, more to the point, how she was going to find it. Lunchtimes were always a flurry of activity inside Miss Peters' Office, and with the torrential rain outside, it was especially busy. As Rose waited to pick her opportunity, a plan began to form in her mind. It wasn't a good plan, depending as it did on Miss Peters' notoriously poor memory, but in the absence of anything better, Rose decided to give it a try.

"Miss, delp de!" she yelped, clutching her face and racing up to the fraught teacher.

"Rose Berry?" scowled Miss Peters, "that's twice you've been here in two days!"

"Miss, delp de!"

Miss Peters' expression changed to one of concern, "What's the matter?"

"Dive deen sdung!"

"Stung?"

"Yes, sdung dye a dosp on dye dose." Rose contorted her face in pain.

"What? You've been stung by a wasp? On a rainy day like this?"

Rose distracted her with another pained yelp, "Aaaaoooowwww!"

"Dear me!" said Miss Peters in panic. "We must get you to the Medical Room."

"Do!" screamed Rose, through covered fingers. "Dime dallergic. Dye musd dav dan dallergy dipe dight dow!"

"What?"

"No! Dye musd dav dan *allergy wipe* dight *now!*" she repeated, ensuring that the essential words were spelled out.

"I haven't got any allergy wipes," said Miss Peters. "You really must go—" then she paused, remembering the wipes she kept in her drawer. "Hadn't Candy said yesterday morning that they were for insect stings?"

Miss Peters thrust her hands into her tight-fitting trouser pockets and, teeth clenched, managed to prise free her keys.

Next, she shunted herself down into her chair and unlocked her desk drawer, yanking it so savagely that it left its frame altogether and became momentarily airborne. It spiralled across the tiny office, clattered against the wall and fell to the floor in a mass of screws and splintering wood. Its contents *would have* scattered everywhere *if* there'd been anything inside it, but there wasn't. Trudy Peters' desk drawer was completely empty.

The bemused teacher gawped at the scene of devastation, "That's strange," she said, "very strange."

Rose miraculously regained her power of speech, "No problem, Miss," she said sheepishly, "I'll go to see Miss Megson in the Medical Room. I'm sure she'll have some wipes. I'll be fine. Thanks, anyway." Then she beat a hasty retreat.

****

Whilst Miss Peters sat looking at her empty drawer, Inky was standing inside a pitch-black vault with Crispin Merridew's file in his hand. He guessed what must have happened: from inside his office, Wiggy had noticed the vault's light switch in the down position, and, assuming he'd left it on by accident, he'd flicked it off and continued about his business.

The Great School Detective shuffled over to his rucksack and quickly located a long, thin torch. Twisting its head clockwise, a funnel of white light spilled out across the cavernous space. By torchlight, the vault adopted a much more sinister atmosphere, but Inky continued undeterred, manoeuvring around Stanley's archives with renewed purpose. Crispin's file, he'd known for some time, would be crucial to solving the case, and only a casual glance at its contents gave him the evidence he needed. He duly slid it into his rucksack, planning to take a closer look later.

But it wasn't just Crispin he was interested in, he needed to dig out other information too, and being securely locked inside the vault, he set about this at a brisk pace.

Half an hour later, Inky had found everything he needed. He now knew both who had taken Fred's keys and why, and he had all the evidence to prove it. If everything went to plan, he expected to have the keys in his possession before the end of the day, but first, he had to conduct a little research of his own.

What Miss Peters had said to him about checking his personal file had been burrowing into his mind ever since, scritching and scratching away like a rat in a drain, and now it was time to confront the matter.

Inky made his way back down the central aisle to the fourth-year section. He swiftly located his own folder and carefully removed it from its crate. He flipped back its cardboard flap and removed the cluster of papers it contained. Because he'd only joined Blinkton halfway through the third-year, his folder was much slimmer than most. Inside, were only a handful of documents: exam papers, a school report, absence notes, a commendation from Mr Carmichael in chemistry and one from Madam Gaudet in French. He flicked though these casually until he found what he was looking for: a small, brown envelope addressed to Miss Peters, the word 'confidential' emblazoned across its front. He unsealed this with great care, gently prising the flap away from its casing. He then slid out the single piece of paper it contained, unfolded it, and began to read:

Mr P Bearon

Chief Resettlement Officer

Sir Thomas Lee Towers

Old Pepper Lane

PO Box 137, Krull

Confidential Memo. Re. Master Stevens

To: Miss Trudy Peters, Head of Year Four, Blinkton High School.

Dear Miss Peters,

As you're already aware, Master Stevens was relocated to Blinkton High School halfway through his third year under traumatic circumstances. At the same time, he was removed

---

from his mother's care with immediate effect and placed under the care of his mother's sister and brother-in-law, Alice and Eric Garner, pending a review of what would be in the young man's best interests moving forwards.

Now that matters have settled down and a degree of stability restored, it's time to reach a more permanent solution concerning the future of Master Stevens. Mr and Mrs Garner have requested that they be allowed to continue caring for their nephew, but we need to consider whether this is the best option to meet his needs. I must inform you, Miss Peters, that as his Head of Year, your opinion in this matter will carry significant weight.

The previous Head of Year, Mr Passaretto, raised several concerns about Master Stevens. He suggested that the young man, although progressing exceedingly well in his studies, was in possession of an aloof and solitary nature. He also commented that Master Stevens refused to conform to the school's dress code and that, although not popular in the conventional sense, he seemed to exert a subversive influence upon his peers.

In short, based on all the evidence at my disposal, I'm concerned that Master Stevens may require a more controlled and specialist environment in which to meet his educational and emotional needs.

Having said this, I have not observed Master Stevens on a day-to-day basis, therefore, I'd be grateful if you could update me further in this matter, as I weigh up all the options for this vulnerable young man.

All information relating to Master Stevens will be treated in the strictest confidence, and swift communication would be appreciated.

Yours sincerely,

Paul Bearon - <u>Chief Resettlement Officer.</u>

Inky's mind spun. Certain phrases leapt out at him from the surface of the torch-lit paper: 'traumatic circumstances', 'solitary nature', 'controlled and specialist environment', 'subversive influence.' He slowly refolded the letter and returned it to its envelope, which he resealed, sticking it back down neatly, before returning it to its folder and placing it back in the appropriate crate.

Just at that moment, without warning, the vault's lights blinked back on and its door flew open, revealing the Statistician beyond.

****

In cookery, Rose supplied an appropriate excuse for Inky's absence. She explained some wild tale to Miss Pinkerton about how he'd been hit in the face by a football at lunchtime and had to be taken to the Medical Room with a bloodied nose.

"No problem," replied Miss Pinkerton, relieved that her pristine cooking equipment was not about to be contaminated.

However, Ross was less successful. In response to Chalky Whittle's enquiry, all Ross could come up with was: "Inky? He's been asked to work on a special history project with Mr Dukes. It's all about Anne Boleyn, Catherine of Aragon and Anne of Cleavage."

"Enough, Berry!" said Whittle with disdain. "I'll check with Mr Dukes later to see if that stack of nonsense holds up." Then he turned to the class: "Right everyone, *Lord of the Flies* – Watkins, can you start reading from page 104, please?"

****

As soon as the strip lights flickered on inside the vault, Inky dived to his right. He snapped off his torch in mid-flight and somehow managed to remain silent, despite a hard landing on the stone floor. Luckily, he was deep enough inside the vault to be hidden within the matrix of shelves, well away from the door that had just swung open.

Inky sat up, feverishly working out his escape. He put his

torch into his backpack, looped this over his arms, then created a spy-hole by gently prising apart two crates. He quickly scanned across to where Stanley's silhouette had appeared at the top of the central aisle. He saw the Statistics Officer carrying a pile of crates stacked one on top of another so high that his face was obscured.

Inky slowly crawled towards the edge of the row he'd found himself hiding in and watched with horror as Stanley tottered in his direction. All he could see were the Statistician's bandy legs, creased trousers and brown Hush Puppies. As Stanley neared, the young detective could plainly hear the croaky rattle at the back of his throat and the scuff of his shoes on the dry, stone floor.

Scuff, scuff, scuff …

Inky readied himself for confrontation, one knee balanced on the floor like a sprinter at the start of a race. He wasn't sure quite what form this confrontation would take, deferring that decision to the second he fell under the old man's gaze, but miraculously that moment never came: Maxwell Stanley wheezed right up to Inky's recess, then carried straight on towards the bowels of the vault, completely oblivious to the detective's presence. With his face pressed directly into his work-crates, the Statistician had continued onwards without so much as a sideways glance, huffing and blowing. This was all the opportunity the young detective needed; he was up and gone, snaking around the shelving unit, down the central aisle and out of the vault altogether.

With the scent of freedom still fresh in his nostrils, Inky tiptoed across the Statistics Office floor and placed a hand on the door handle, only to find it stuck. He tried again a little harder, but the result was the same, the door wouldn't give; it was locked.

From the chamber beyond the iron door came the sound of a hefty grunt and boxes being placed down onto the stone floor one at a time. This was followed by sound of shoes scuffing their way back across the flagstones:

Scuff, scuff, scuff …

The detective looked around in desperation. He noticed Stanley's jacket and gown draped over the back of his office chair and guessed that his keys were likely to be inside the pockets, but there wasn't time to find the relevant pocket or the relevant key to unlock the outside door. Only seconds away from discovery and devoid of other ideas, Inky took the only option available to him: he raced over to the vault's iron door, kicked it shut, inserted the key and turned it clockwise with a reassuring click.

"Hey!" came a cry, which lost intensity as the door slammed in on it. Inky leaned back against the door and swept aside the curl that had fallen over his eyes. He didn't feel proud of what he'd done, but told himself that sometimes the end justified the means.

Time was now a luxury and the detective set about making a rapid escape. Stanley's jacket did indeed yield his keys, but Inky also discovered something else, something entirely unexpected: there, sitting in a heap on top of the desk, was a fluffy clump of plastic-looking hair. Out of politeness, Inky concealed Stanley's toupee inside a desk drawer before unlocking the door and then placing the office keys back inside his jacket pocket. He then stepped out into the rain-drenched yard, making a mental note to ask Ginny Cartwright to organise the Statistician's release.

****

By the time Inky finally emerged, there were just ten minutes to the end of school. Even in the short time he'd been absent from class, the storm had intensified. Raindrops the size of marbles swept across the yard, bouncing off the tarmac and giving the impression of steam rising. Great curtains of water were driven on by fierce squalls. Inky had only ten minutes until his rendezvous with Ross and Rose, but where could he go to keep dry until then? He needed to distance himself from the Statistics Office. The chalky staleness at the base of the spiral staircase beckoned; at least it was dry there. Inky swept across the yard, water splashing around his ankles. On reaching the weathered door, he quickly coiled a hand around its handle and pulled, but for the second time that day, he found a door that wouldn't move. He tried again, this time applying a second hand and his full bodyweight, but the door held fast. Someone had used Fred's missing keys to lock it, and Inky knew exactly who that was.

Stranded and at the mercy of the elements, Inky plumped for the second-best option: he paddled around the corner and took advantage of what little shelter there was beneath the arch itself. He leaned back against its damp stonework, wrapped his arms around himself, and remained motionless, lost in thought, hidden behind a screen of cascading water.

However, the investigator's reverie was quickly broken by a series of musical notes, which were clearly audible above the sound of the downpour. Inky took a step back and watched with interest as Fred Varley appeared around the corner of the Languages Department, whistling. The old man was little more than a dark blur through all the rain, but it was unquestionably him. Fred pulled open his door sharply and disappeared inside, his movement stiff, shoulders hunched.

No sooner had Fred disappeared than Perry Dukes raced into view. Bounding up to the Maintenance Room door, jacket held high above his head, he pummelled on Fred's door. There was no reply. Dukes knocked again, soaked and impatient, but there was still no response. He tried the handle, but it refused to budge. Minutes later, with the rain staining his suit black and the home-time bell ringing, Dukes decided to beat a hasty retreat, before getting caught up in the early-evening exodus.

CHAPTER EIGHTEEN –
THE READING CLUB

Ross and Rose were among the home-time stampede that Peregrine Dukes was keen to avoid. On catching sight of Inky sheltering beneath the arch, the pair peeled away from the general flow to join their classmate.

"Have you found out who took Fred's keys?" said Ross, without greeting.

"Where are they?" asked Rose, appearing at her brother's shoulder.

"Now's not the time. Let's find shelter so you can tell me what you've observed this afternoon," said Inky, heading back into school against the tide of escaping children.

The trio eventually battled their way to the Languages Department cloakroom where they flopped down on a wooden bench.

"So, you managed to get out of Wiggy's office in one piece?" said Rose.

"Just about," said Inky, "but before I explain, please tell me about Crispin and Candy."

"There's not much to say," said Ross, "Crispin's been his usual self, swinging his satchel around. I've seen nothing to suggest that he's the culprit."

"The same can be said of Candy," said Rose. "I saw nothing out of the ordinary in her behaviour, although we can't rule her out. I did as you asked, I fooled Miss Peters into unlocking her desk drawer and it was empty – the make-up she'd confiscated yesterday had gone, so perhaps Candy took Fred's keys to retrieve it?"

Inky didn't respond.

"One thing's for certain," added Ross, "Whitkirk has no motive for taking the keys; he's left Blinkton for good."

"Talking of staff," said Rose, "Perry was looking for you. When he couldn't find you, he asked me to pass on a message. He said that, even if you leave it until the very last minute, you must help Fred if you find anything at all. He even suggested that you could interrupt the Snake's meeting with Fred tomorrow!"

The twins looked across at the detective for a response, but his eyes gave nothing away. All he did was invite them to follow him once more, this time leading them back to the school's main staircase. "We're going to do some reading," he said.

The trio climbed up two flights and arrived outside Room 8, where Desmond 'Fluff' Charlton, Head of English, was hosting his weekly Reading Club.

Inky quickly led the twins to the room next door where he thumped down a folder onto a table, "I'd like you to examine Crispin's student file. It's a record of everything he's achieved at Blinkton. I took it from Wiggy's vault."

"Blimey, it's thick!" said Rose.

"You stole it?" said Ross.

"I intend to return it, but I was meant to find it," Inky replied. "It was placed, very deliberately, in an area where the perpetrator knew I'd be searching for it. It literally fell down on top of me." He slid the file across the table, and Rose flipped it open. Inside was an assortment of papers, which the twins shuffled through in awe.

"Have you seen how many commendations there are?" said Ross.

"But it's these papers that are significant," said Inky, and from the pile he extracted Crispin's end-of-year exam papers and fanned them in the way a croupier might present a deck of cards. "Study them carefully, but hurry up!"

The Berrys set about their task. Ross noted the pencil-written scores at the top of each paper, "I don't believe it!" he said. "Crispin's scored one hundred per cent in every subject. It's incredible!"

"I agree," said Inky, "But you've missed something: Crispin did not always score full marks. Look at the papers again closely."

"Ah yes," said Rose, pointing to the science paper, "there's a single cross, right there."

"There are others too," said Inky, rifling through the papers. "Not many, admittedly. It seems the marks written at the top of each paper don't tally with his actual scores."

"So, what?" shrugged Rose. "Crispin gets a couple of questions wrong. He scores ninety-eight per cent, instead of a hundred. Big deal!"

"Come on, Rose," said Ross, "think about it! Think about what happened at Drama Club. Getting full marks must matter an awful lot to someone like Crispin."

"So, stealing the caretaker's keys was all about Crispin being able to cheat his test scores," said Rose. "And," she added as an afterthought, "get his hands on a chess set."

"That's what we've been led to believe," said Inky. "If you examine the numbers carefully, you can still see Crispin's original marks, the ones that have been rubbed out and rewritten. The traces are faint, but detectable nevertheless. And you'll also notice that the replacement marks are all written in the same handwriting."

Ross sat back, "That's terrible. But it's also disturbing that Lord Merridew puts so much pressure on his son that he resorts to cheating. I feel for Fred, but I feel sorry for Crispin too. If he thinks that ninety-nine per cent is a failure, then he has a serious problem."

Inky stood up sharply, "I'm glad you're so understanding, Ross, because it's you who is going to retrieve Fred's keys. They'll be inside Crispin's satchel next door, and I need you to recover them. You're the one who's struck up a rapport with him, after all."

Ross stood up awkwardly, "Inky, I barely know Crispin."

But the detective's eyes were alive with mischief, "Improvise! We'll be waiting here to hear news of your success."

****

Ross noticed that his hand was trembling as he placed it on the door handle of Room 8. Having only had a few minutes to concoct some crazy story, he burst into the Reading Club: "Right, everyone, out! It's a fire drill. Fire!" he shouted, so loudly that he started to cough.

Fluff was the first on his feet, his voice rich after so many years' teaching, "Is this some kind of prank? Why are we having a fire drill outside school hours and in this weather?"

"It's the Snake's orders," Ross pleaded. "She said we needed the practice. Please could everybody make their way outside to the assembly point in the yard?"

Hoping to speed things along, Ross adopted a position by the door and gestured outside.

No one moved. Members of the Reading Club looked from one to another in confusion, the storm hammering against the window only adding to their reluctance to leave.

Finally, Fluff gave way, "Come on, everyone!" he announced. "Can we all make our way outside into the yard?" As the class began to stir, he glared at Ross, one eye hidden behind a cascade of silver hair, "Young man, if I find that this is a hoax, you will be in serious trouble."

"All of you!" barked Ross, relieved to see a response. Then, to his horror, he saw Crispin heading towards the stack of school bags. "Please leave your bags where they are. Everyone must make their way out to the assembly point leaving all *possessions behind!*"

Ross ushered the members of the Reading Club out of Room 8. As they passed, they thrust battered copies of *Hamlet* at him angrily. Crispin Merridew was the only student to show any kindness, hanging back after the others had left. "Hi, Ross! Great acting, by the way," he said with a wink. "You're a natural.

You should sign up for Miss Birkin's show after Christmas."

"I think my acting talents are wearing a bit thin," said Ross, unable to shake his feeling of disappointment in the youngster.

"No problem, Ross. See you around."

No sooner had Crispin closed the door than Ross dashed across to the soggy cluster of school bags heaped in the corner. Crispin's satchel was easy to locate, nestling towards the bottom of the stack. Ross unbuckled its straps guiltily, flung it open, and began to sift through its contents.

****

"Excellent work," Inky said, when Ross returned.

"Will I get into trouble?"

"Probably, but it's Fred's career that's at stake, and which is more important?" said Rose. "Did you find the keys?"

Ross removed his hand from behind his back to reveal a fistful of clanking metal. "They were at the bottom of Crispin's satchel," he said flatly.

Inky was swift to relieve his classmate of the pickings. "Task accomplished, Master Berry," he said, bundling the bunch into his rucksack and patting down its leather flap.

****

Outside, as the storm raged on, the young detective led the twins away from school, avoiding the spot where the members of the Reading Club were assembled. Great squalls picked up crumpled cans and flung them about the yard like shrapnel. Rose tried to put up an umbrella, but soon gave up for fear of it being turned inside out. Ross pulled the hood of his parka tightly around his face.

As the trio passed Fred's Maintenance Room, Ross pulled up and shouted above the downpour, "Shouldn't we give the keys back to Fred, if he's still in there? He'll be worried sick."

But Inky pressed on.

"Come on, Inky," said Rose, "tell us how you knew that Crispin did it!"

"I never said that Crispin did it," he said bluntly.

"But the keys were inside his satchel. I caught him red-handed," said Ross. "He changed his exam scores – you showed us the proof."

"And Crispin likes chess and the thief stole a chess set," added Rose.

"At no time did I ever state that Crispin was the thief," said Inky, "or that he changed his exam scores." He turned his porcelain face, slick with rain, towards her, "I said that that was what we've been led to believe. We've been following a trail laid out for us by the real culprit."

"So, if it wasn't Crispin, who was it?" asked Rose.

"That," said the detective, angling his face into the swirling blackness, "is the all-important question. One which will be addressed before Fred meets the Snake tomorrow."

A flash of lightning somewhere out over the sea gave Inky's face a ghostly sheen. "It's a complicated game, and you have both been a great help, but it's my turn to make the next move. I'll explain everything in due course. But now I need time to focus. Go home, both of you, dry yourselves off and rest up for the evening."

Inky flicked up his collar and set off along the deserted street. Ross made to go after him, but Rose caught hold of her brother's arm, "Let him go," she said. "He's made up his mind; we can't help him any further."

The pair watched Inky depart along a mirror of rainwater. Then, they set off for home, battling through the rain like a pair of Arctic explorers.

CHAPTER NINETEEN –
THE DARKENING

"I need you to look at this, please, Uncle Eric," announced Inky, sweeping into the Garner's front room with water dripping from his coat and dampening the carpet.

"Hello, Son," replied Eric Garner, bleary-eyed. "Blimey, you're like a drowned rat!"

"Please, could you look at this?" Inky repeated.

"Of course," said Eric, shuffling into an upright position and turning the television down. "Pass me my reading glasses, would you?"

Inky crouched down at his uncle's side. He unbuckled his rucksack and handed over a document onto which a passport-sized photograph had been clipped, "You watch the local news every night, don't you, Uncle?" he said.

"Most nights. I was about to watch it just now."

"Is this anyone you recognise? From the news?"

Eric put on his glasses, unclipped the photograph and moved it back and forwards in front of his eyes until he achieved focus. The picture showed a man's face in black and white, staring back with a menacing expression.

"Sorry, Son," said Eric, "I can't place him. I'm normally good with faces, but I've drawn a blank with that one. Is it important?"

He handed the photograph back to Inky, leaned back and laced his hands behind his head.

"How about now?" Inky said, thrusting the photograph forwards once more, but this time with the bottom half covered so that only half the man's face was on show.

Eric leaned forwards again, deep in concentration. "Hang on a minute!" he said, "I do recall him, but I'm going back a few years." Eric scratched his head.

"What was his name? Come on, Uncle Eric, think!"

Eric thought for some time before finally producing a name. It was not the name Inky had expected; not quite. Same person; different name, but once it had left his uncle's lips, everything made sense.

Eric continued, "Nasty piece of work, too, as I recall. Created quite a stir along the coast. Armed robbery it was. He and his brother were both involved, but the brother got let off. How did you get hold of this photograph, Son? I hope you're not involved in anything to do with that bloke."

"Don't worry, Uncle Eric. I'm just interested in the criminal mind," said Inky, and he took back the photograph and darted upstairs.

Eric Garner leaned back and turned the television up. From the screen, the words 'SEVERE WEATHER WARNING' flashed back at him in alternating red and black lettering. Eric moved over to the window and pulled back the curtains warily, before being disturbed by a shrill command:

"Eric, can you come in here, quick? I think I've burned something!"

****

Thirty minutes later Eric and Alice Garner were standing side by side at the sink, covered in soapsuds, when they became aware of Inky's presence. He was standing in the doorway with his coat on, his face partially lost to shadow.

"Sorry, Love, I didn't see you there. It'll be scrambled eggs on crumpets for tea tonight, I'm afraid."

"You'll have to excuse me, but I have something to attend to," Inky replied. "I'll be back as soon as I can. Please, don't wait up."

"But the weather!" protested Alice, "It's not safe, Love. There's warnings on the news. They're telling everyone not to venture out except in an emergency."

"I'll be home before you know it," Inky said.

Eric was not reassured. "If this has anything to do with that bloke in the photo, Inky—"

"Don't worry, Uncle Eric. Trust me. This is important, not just for others, but for us as a family. I'll be back soon, I promise."

"*Us as a family*" – Inky's words echoed through Alice's mind. It was the first time, he'd referred to them as 'family', and she felt uplifted.

Inky fastened his coat, its buttons stiff against the damp leather, adjusted the straps on his rucksack and strode outside.

As the front door closed, the Garners moved over to the window to watch as Inky disappeared down the road, bent double by the force of the wind. Alice sighed heavily. The child they'd begged to be allowed to care for had left the cheery warmth of their home to confront some mysterious injustice on the wildest of nights. "I worry about him," she said, removing the tea-towel from her shoulder. "Why can't he be like other teenagers? I know he's been through a lot, but can't he just be *normal* now?"

Eric supplied a reassuring arm, "You know very well that no teenager is ever 'normal'. I certainly wasn't normal at his age."

Alice looked at him questioningly.

"And despite Inky's little …" he struggled for the word, "*eccentricities*, he's a fine young man. He's a bit introverted, I know, but he more than makes up for that with the wisdom he possesses."

"True."

"So, we should trust him, Love. He has a special gift. He *is* special. We're lucky to have him."

"But the Council could decide to take him away."

"They won't, I promise," said Eric. "They know he's happy and safe with us. And while they take their time deliberating, we must give him all the support he needs, even if it involves turning a blind eye to some of his," he flung out a hand, "*peculiar* activities."

"But what if he gets into trouble?"

"He won't. *Our* Inky can take care of himself. He'll be back soon, safe and sound."

Eric Garner sank into an uneasy silence, hoping he'd managed to sound more confident than he felt.

Outside, a bolt of lightning cracked overhead throwing Inky and the cherry tree on the corner into sharp silhouette. As the young detective passed the sapling, it swayed down towards him, bent almost double by the force of the wind. It looked, for all the world, as if the tree was stooping down to talk to him.

****

The Great School Detective made his way through deserted streets down to the harbour, impervious to the tempest swirling around him. At the sea wall, he stood alone on its promontory and breathed in deeply, tasting the salt on his lips, drinking in the many flavours of the storm. Sprays of salt water lashed his face causing his skin to tingle. The sea, which spread itself out in front of him, was a vast cooking pot, which bubbled and boiled – a cauldron of roiling blackness. Sparks of lightning detonated on the horizon one after another, briefly bleaching the undersides of the clouds, before fading back to black.

Inky shuffled out of his rucksack, reached inside and removed the mass of keys from within, his grip so tight on the sharp metal that it left indentations in his palm.

CHAPTER TWENTY –
THUNDER CLAP

Blinkton School rose against the evening sky like a tombstone. With the moon held captive behind tumbling clouds, Inky's outline was barely visible against its imposing bulk. He stood motionless, watching the rain as it lashed against brick, steel and glass. A camera flash of lightning momentarily bleached the brickwork before sliding back into shiny, rain-soaked blackness. The resulting crash of thunder built from a tinny rumble into a full-throated roar in seconds. The detective took a step forwards, pushed open the unlocked door and disappeared inside.

Having entered the Reception, Inky became aware of the silence that seemed to carpet the entire building – heavy and foreboding. Suddenly, another flash of lightning detonated – magnesium light dazzled off polished chrome, dizzying and blinding, before being engulfed by the blackness once more.

Inky waited for his eyes to readjust, feeling as if some giant beast had just awoken – as if the building itself had somehow lumbered into life. Unable to shake the feeling of being watched, he located his torch and snapped it on; specks of dust immediately swirled within its beam like a miniature snowstorm.

Inky angled the light down at his feet and set about his task. First, he perched on Ginny Cartwright's chair and flipped through her telephone log, cross-checking all the calls made to the Reception whilst Fred had been repairing the electric sockets the previous Friday. He ran a finger down each entry in turn:

2:06.	Miss Sheldon. Music. Sent for Miss Megson for medical assistance. Davey Wyndham choking on euphonium mouthpiece.
2:17.	Mrs Morris. Textiles. Request for assistance to deal with Alex Horton, who's sewn Jeremiah Serlin's trouser legs together.
2:34.	Mr Spencer. Games. Requested an order from the Codfather: Fish and chips with mushy peas and extra scraps.
2:47.	Miss Pinkerton. Cookery. Crispin Merridew given permission to go to Reflection Room.

Altercation with Bridie McMuffin and Kristy Gee.

3:04. Mr Webster. Playground duty. Request for senior staff assistance. Spud Barton hit Noel Smith over the head with a plastic ruler.

Satisfied, Inky closed the ledger and repositioned it as he'd found it. He then approached the Snake's Office.

Even by torchlight the room exuded a sense of luxury. The carpet was charcoal-grey, fresh-smelling and soft underfoot. Up ahead, the far wall was made from a single piece of mirrored glass, and the blinds were open so that a majestic old oak was visible outside in silhouette. Its branches beat time with the wildness of the wind, as if conducting the storm with a hundred gnarly batons.

On the right-hand wall hung a framed portrait of Geoffrey Williams, Blinkton's longest serving headmaster. The long-dead tyrant gazed down at the intruder with an expression of disdain. A large beechwood desk dominated the central area; its highly polished surface was bare except for a half-drunk coffee and a copy of *Women's Weekly*. Positioned beyond this was the Snake's chair, made of soft, padded leather, with eight different recliner settings. But Inky had no time to admire such luxury; he scanned the room quickly in search of a place to deposit the item he'd brought.

With his task completed, Inky switched off his torch and retraced his steps to the Reception. The Snake's door closed behind him, relocking with an expensive-sounding clunk. Inky let out a sigh and then headed towards the entrance door and the storm that raged outside. He hadn't gone more than a few steps when suddenly the room shook with a deafening *BOOM*.

To Inky, it seemed that the world had suddenly exploded. A forked bolt of lightning speared into the playground, striking the oak tree with a cacophonous roar. The tree's trunk was immediately ripped in half and several boughs were wrenched clean off, embedding themselves into the sodden grass. The deafening squeal of splintering wood wrenched the air, while leaves scattered beneath like playing cards. Inky's eyes streamed and everything lost shape, as though he'd stared directly into the sun. Then, as his vision slowly returned, a shadow emerged out of the whiteness, striding towards him.

"Stevens! Fancy meeting you here!" the figure said, raising an arm.

The last thing Inky saw was a piece of wood hanging in the air, which swept down in a violent arc. Then everything went black ...

CHAPTER TWENTY-ONE – PRESSURE MOUNTING

Inky regained consciousness with a groan; he'd been out cold for some time. His head throbbed and the back of his throat was dry. His arms were pinned to his sides by thick coils of rope, tied so tightly they bit into his flesh. At once, he realised with sickening clarity where he was and what had happened to him.

"I always suspected it was you," Inky said to the figure standing in front of him.

"You're too smart for your own good, Stevens," came the reply, "but you're not looking quite so clever now, are you?"

The figure continued, "I'd heard a lot about you, Stevens. 'The Great School Detective' sounded ideal for what I had in mind. 'I'll be able to manipulate this kid; use him for my own purposes,' I thought."

"But things haven't played out as you expected, have they?" said Inky, the smell of engine oil flooding his nostrils. "You've achieved nothing."

The man grabbed hold of Inky by the hair, wild-eyed and vicious, "I have other options. There's still time. This is just a setback."

The man threw Inky's head forwards causing a stab of pain to erupt at the base of his neck, but Inky continued: "You'll fail again, Vincent Arley," he said, pausing to let his words sink in. "You're pathetic. I didn't know who you were at the start, but I saw the initials 'VA' stitched onto your handkerchief, and I've done my research. Frederick Varley doesn't exist, does he? You're a fraud!"

The man landed a punch into the young detective's midriff, which left him gulping for air, each heave of his chest causing his restraints to cut deeper.

When Inky's convulsions subsided, he surveyed his surroundings once more. "What am I tied to?" he asked.

"This little thing here?" said Arley, slapping a palm onto the metal cylinder behind him with a dull *clang*. "Inky Stevens," he said with amusement, "I'd like to introduce you to Betty! She's cute eh? This little beauty heats up the entire school. She's dependable, but she does tend to leak and blow off steam, and she can become very, very hot!"

Arley laughed so forcefully that he had to lean up against the pipework to steady himself. All traces of the meek, browbeaten caretaker had gone. He regained his composure and locked eyes with his captive, "It's time for some entertainment, Stevens. And don't get any silly ideas about attracting attention; there's no one to hear you. Besides," he held up his bunch of keys like an angler showing off a prized catch, "the keys to this little nook are now in my possession."

Arley opened his hand and let the clump of metal drop onto cracked concrete. "So," he said, "it's time to start talking!"

"What makes you think I'll talk?"

Arley rushed forwards and seized Inky's chin between his thumb and forefinger, "I don't *think* you'll talk, Stevens," he spat, "I *know* you'll talk, because by the time Old Betty gets fired up, you'll scream what I want to know from the top of your lungs."

Arley swept over to the doorway and took hold of a metal lever, "I'm feeling chilly, aren't you? Shall we turn up the heat a little?" Arley dropped the handle, and immediately, the huge slab of metal behind Inky started to shudder, its vibrations causing the rope around him to grip even tighter. Betty had awoken.

After her initial quaking, the boiler settled into a rhythmic whirr as her old pumps pushed slowly-heating water through the school's ageing pipework.

Inky swallowed, his throat raw.

Arley crouched down, "Look at this, Stevens!"

At floor level, three symmetrical valves were arranged in a row, each topped with a circular handle and welded onto a metal pipe. Arley shut each one off in turn, fighting against ingrained rust, and then wiped his hands down the sides of his jacket, "That ought to do it, eh? Hot work, but not nearly as hot as you're about to get! Now listen, Stevens. I won't insult you; I think you're clever enough to work out for yourself what's going to happen. Betty's all bunged up, so it's only a matter of time before something *explosive* happens; it might take as little as thirty minutes, or perhaps an hour, who knows? But one thing's for certain, that boiler's going to become warm, then excruciatingly hot, and then," he mimed an explosion with his hands, "she's gonna blow!"

Inky felt a sick feeling in the pit of his stomach.

"And when she does blow," he grinned, "I won't be around to hear it."

Arley's sentence swirled in the hot air. It had only been a matter of minutes yet Inky could already feel the heat warming through his coat. "Why are you still here, Arley?" he said. "What do you want?"

"I want to see you to suffer, Stevens. But also," he added, "I want answers."

Arley paced the room with a confidence never displayed by his alter-ego. He looked different. He spoke differently.

For a moment, Arley disappeared behind the boiler, and when he re-emerged, he was clutching a beer crate in one hand and an object wrapped in cloth in the other. He set the wooden crate down and sat on it, facing the teenager.

"You've made things difficult for me, Stevens. I thought all was going to plan, but when you arrived here tonight, you spoiled everything. So, in the brief time you have left, I'd like you to tell me what you know and where I went wrong – to help me avoid making mistakes in future. Or," he let the cloth fall to the floor to reveal a sawn-off shotgun tucked into his body, "I could just blow your head off now?"

Blood rushed to Inky's cheeks, and he could feel his head start to swim.

"You went wrong," he began, "because you made too many mistakes, starting with your bungled robbery."

"Ah yes, the robbery! That wasn't a mistake; just an unfortunate accident. My shotgun jammed and I got caught. That was all."

Inky continued undeterred. "But your brother was found innocent and freed without charge."

"Clive was found innocent because he was innocent. I

forced him to help me."

"We both know there was more to it than that. Clive Arley, or *Clive Sugarcane* as he's now known, has been helping you ever since your release. I find that strange, unless he owes you something?" Inky's words continued hot and breathy, "You see, I studied your file in the school vault and Candy's too. The address you gave on your job application matches hers. You live with your brother and niece. You even talk the *bloomin'* same."

Beneath his beard, Arley's jaw tightened.

Inky went on, "Clive gave you a roof over your head to repay the debt for you keeping him out of prison. Clive and Carly, as she used to be called, had managed to build a new life for themselves after your robbery fiasco. They moved away from Plumpton Sands to Blinkton-on-Sea, another deadbeat seaside town – nice and anonymous. And while you counted down the days inside, father and daughter established themselves as members of Blinkton society. But when you were released from prison, everything changed, didn't it?"

"You're good, Stevens. Go on."

"When you moved into Clive's house, all three of you were forced to change names so that no one would spot the connection."

Arley made a show of clapping his hands, "Breaking into

Blinkton's vault to check up on me? I admire your pluck, Stevens. I'll be almost sorry to see you go."

"You think strapping me to a stick of dynamite's the answer to your problems? You'll never get away with it."

"Really?" Arley spoke to the room at large, like a lawyer addressing a jury. "An unseasonably violent storm … A bolt of lightning hits Blinkton School … Its decrepit boiler explodes taking half the building with it, plus you too, of course, Stevens. It's all so *bloomin'* fortuitous, M'lord." Arley's smile cut through his tangled beard, "Now," he said, easing himself back down onto the crate, "if you recall, I asked you to tell me where you think I went wrong."

"Revenge," said Inky, raising his voice over the clanking pipes. "Revenge was your mistake."

Arley feigned surprise. "On whom?"

Inky eyed his adversary coldly, "Lord Merridew, that's who!"

"Lord Merridew, eh?"

"Stop playing dumb! This whole charade about your supposedly missing keys was designed to disgrace Lord Merridew. You wanted to discredit him by humiliating his son."

"Now why would I want to do that?" Arley sneered. "Because he laughed at my attempt to mend a coffee machine?"

"No, because Marmaduke Merridew was the High Court

Judge who sent you to prison ten years ago – '*Him with the pinstripe suit and bloomin' bowler hat*'. You're sick, Arley – looking to blame someone else for your own contemptible actions."

A shadow crossed Arley's face.

Inky continued, "Your shoddy work around school shows you're not a real caretaker, but working here as a handyman was the only position open to you. And it was essential you came to work here, because it's here that Lord Merridew's most precious commodity, his only son, would be accessible to you."

Arley leapt to his feet, nostrils flaring.

"You didn't know what shape your revenge would take," persisted Inky. "But you were content to bide your time until an opportunity presented itself. And that opportunity finally arrived last Friday. While you were hacking away at electric sockets, a distressed young lad entered the Reflection Room, and your sick mind began to scheme. By Monday morning, you'd concocted this whole plan to frame Crispin for stealing your keys and thereby embarrass the man who put you away. The Crown Court Judge with a thief and a cheat for a son; it would strike Lord Merridew's heart. He'd never be able to forgive Crispin."

"Yes, Stevens, but this doesn't sound like a mistake to me;

Merridew had it coming to him. Sitting there with his silly wig on, making decisions that change people's lives – that changed *my* life. Ten years. *Ten years!*" In a fit of temper, Arley kicked the crate and watched it skitter across the floor, slamming up against the rusty pipework.

A flicker of reasoning told Inky that he needed to keep Arley's attention. "Getting me to do your dirty work was another mistake," he said. "I could see right through you. Even when you described the vault key, right at the beginning, I had my suspicions. You were too precise; too specific about this 'ornate key with a filigree handle'. And when this item just happened to turn up, I found myself asking, 'why this one and not any of the others?' You even mentioned the Statistics Office."

Inky's tongue felt thick in his mouth, and beads of sweat ran down his back, but he knew he had to keep on going, "You said you had already searched the Reflection Room, gently steering me into doing a better job myself, and you knew that when I did, I'd be thorough enough to find the key you'd planted inside the Harmony Tent and that I'd be curious enough to find out what it opened and go scampering off in search of evidence."

"Oh, you're good, Stevens. Getting warmer by the second."

"But before hiding the vault key, you needed to use it

yourself. Inside the vault, you placed Crispin's folder on top of the second-year crate making it easier for me to find. That was just too obvious, Arley. You should have made me work harder."

Inky blew sweat away from his cracked lips. By now, hot steam was jetting out from joints in the pipework. It puffed up all around the Boiler Room in thick white clouds.

Inky could feel himself fading. He swallowed hard and forced himself to focus, "It was you who changed the marks on Crispin's exam paper to create some motive for him to want to steal your keys. As if his results weren't good enough already! Same thing with the chess set. I told you that Crispin liked chess so you staged a fake robbery. You even underlined the words 'complete chess set' in your stupid note to me," Inky snorted, "Did you really expect me to believe that Crispin would break into the Common Room after school to steal something so trivial?"

Arley did not respond. Instead, he dragged the gun-barrel across the pipework like a schoolboy trailing a stick across railings.

Inky forced himself on: "And in the Common Room, you claimed to have been attacked by the thief from behind, yet you had a bump on your forehead, conveniently matching a dent in the games cupboard, at *head-height*. You head-butted it yourself, didn't you?"

Arley's eyes flashed. His finger slipped onto the trigger, "Listen to yourself, Stevens. Think you know it all?"

Inky battled on through the heat, "But unfortunately for you, while I was in the vault hunting out information on Crispin, I did some detective work of my own. I read Candy's and Whitkirk's documents, and yours too. I discovered where you lived, that *Frederick Varley* arrived in Blinkton just after Vincent Arley had been released from prison, and that your references were fake. Crucially," his breath emerged hot and dry, "there was a passport-sized photograph of you clipped on to your documents. Someone with a long memory was always going to recognise you."

By now, the room had become filled with swirling clouds of vapour. Inky briefly lost sight of Arley through the steam, his opponent drifting in and out of focus among the intense heat.

"Betty appears to be coming to the boil, Stevens," said, Arley, standing up. "You're lucky that that coat of yours is so thick. It's the only thing keeping you from becoming kebab meat."

Inky summoned up the last of his strength: "You're pathetic," he said. "Despite claiming to have no keys, you still locked the door to Broker's Arch to prevent the Snake becoming too suspicious, didn't you? You also locked Mr Dukes out of your Maintenance Room. You had a plan, but couldn't stick to it.

More mistakes. But your biggest mistake was to implicate your niece. Candy wasn't in the Reflection Room last Friday at all, was she?"

Through the mist, Inky saw Arley hold up his hands in surrender, "You've got me again, Stevens."

"You had to produce an extra suspect to give me more of a challenge.

Arley moved towards the door, aware that the Boiler Room had now started to shake. The sound of crumpling metal snagged the air on a loop.

"I checked the school's phone records on Reception," Inky continued, dizzy with heat and dehydration, "You said you'd telephoned Miss Cartwright about Candy's conduct while she was in the Reflection Room, but her log book shows no such call."

Arley's lip curled into a grimace."

"But you can't control Candy, can you? When Miss Peters confiscated her make-up, she was furious and demanded that you get it all back for her. That wasn't part of your plan, but then what choice did you have? Easier to give in than let her kick up a high-heeled fuss."

Inky paused, struggling to control the pain now searing across his back, but before Arley could respond, the room suddenly shook with the force of an earthquake. Plaster crumbled to dust. Lightning-bolt cracks tore along the walls, ceiling and floor. Pipework ripped. Rivets exploded. Vincent Arley seized hold of the doorframe and clung on to it, terrified.

When equilibrium finally returned, both captor and victim eyed one another white in face. Arley made no attempt to hide his fear and edged back slowly into the safety of the stairwell. From there, he cautiously backed up towards the room above, testing each step before deciding to trust it, "I've enjoyed our little chat, Stevens," he said, "but it's time for me to go."

Suddenly, a pipe ruptured directly above the door. Serrated metal speared across the exit and a jet of steam vomited the full length of the room. Arley scrambled up another couple of stairs.

Inky scanned the smog for a glimpse of his tormentor. His mind whirled, and reeling with fear, pain and fatigue, he channelled his last drop of energy into the only avenue he had available to him, "Go now, Arley," he shouted, "and it's all over!"

Arley cupped a hand to his ear.

"You saw me!" yelled Inky in desperation. "You saw me leave the Snake's Office. It's locked, but I left a letter on her desk. I've told her everything – about you – about Lord Merridew. If I'm finished, so are you; you'll be going down for the rest of your miserable life!"

Arley stood on the stairs only a couple of paces away from safety. He looked down at Inky's limp form tethered below. "I'll grab your note on my way out," he said. "Good of you to let me know."

"You'll find that difficult," Inky said, "Without the key to the Snake's Office. You'll notice it's not on the bunch you took from me."

Arley froze, trapped by indecision: it would be madness not to get out while he could, but what if the kid wasn't bluffing? If there really was a letter, he needed to intercept it. He needed that key.

Inky heard the fury in Arley's movements, as he hurriedly set the shotgun against the disintegrating pipework and leapt down the steps into the Boiler Room, where he started to paw among the steam on the floor. Panicked, desperate and frightened, his fingertips finally alighted on the discarded keys. He quickly scooped them up and clicked them around its stainless-steel ring, several at a time, fingers trembling. Finally, purple with rage, he sat back on his haunches, threw his head back and yelled into the roar of the steam:

"STEEEVENNSSS!"

Arley hurled the keys to the ground and booted them away in frustration, then waded through pools of oily water to the far side of the room. Frantic, he reached up and grabbed hold of the lever and yanked it downwards. In the same movement, he stooped to reopen the circular valves.

"AARRGGGHHH!" he shrieked, as hot metal dials stung the palms of his hands.

The atmosphere inside the Boiler Room began to change, slowly at first, then with surprising speed. The sound of escaping steam faded, and with hot water no longer surging along creaky pipework, Betty's convulsions soon faded from quakes to only the slightest of vibrations.

Boots sploshing, Vincent Arley charged upstairs into the Maintenance Room and returned moments later clutching a chainsaw. He ripped its starter cord, and the machine spluttered into life; metal teeth spun in a savage blur, sparks flew and the stench of diesel fumes filled the room.

Arley hauled the machine high up into the air and disappeared behind Old Betty. One by one, Inky's restraints fell to the floor, unhooked from top to bottom like the back of some giant bodice. Now unsupported, Inky fell forwards, collapsing onto the pieces of frayed rope below. His breathing was shallow and laboured. "Water," he gasped.

"Not now, Stevens," said Arley, "I want that letter! Where's the key?"

"I don't have it."

Arley picked up his shotgun, pointed it down at Inky's head

and closed one eye, "Right, Stevens, I'm going to give you until the count of three—"

"It's in the Reception," Inky stammered.

"Get up!" Arley barked, grabbing his torch from his jacket pocket. "Take me to that key! But I warn you, one false move and you'll feel a lot more than heat spreading across your shoulders!"

Inky staggered to his feet, disorientated and thirsty. Swaying like a punch-drunk boxer, he discreetly brushed the back of his hand across his trouser pocket, reassured to feel the faint outline of the key it contained. Arley hadn't thought to search the detective himself.

"Stop dawdling!" Arley growled and ushered his victim up the stairs into the Maintenance Room, then out into the yard. From there, Inky was forced to re-enter the main body of the school via a side door. He paused to lean up against Lionel Roebuck's statue for support.

"I didn't tell you to stop!" snarled Arley, blinding Inky with his torch. "Hurry up!"

Inky was directed up towards the Reception, the twin barrels of Arley's weapon never leaving his back. His head throbbed and his body was bruised, but it was thirst which pained him most.

The pair finally arrived at the Reception, and Inky slumped

down onto Ginny Cartwright's chair. After the thundering violence of the boiler room, the hush of the Reception felt eerily quiet, as if the space itself was holding its breath. A distant rumble of thunder revealed that the storm had moved on; gone to unleash its fury elsewhere. Inky licked his lips, mesmerised by the rainwater outside. He watched as trickles snaked their way down the freshly polished glass of the entrance doors.

Arley leered, the light casting up from his torch giving his face an otherworldly appearance, his beard glowing silver like wire wool. "Now, Stevens, where's that key?" he growled.

Inky shrank back, "I hid it there," he lied, "beneath the desk."

"Get out of the way! I'll find it." Arley aimed his torch up against the far wall. "Stand over there, and don't try anything silly!"

Inky hobbled over to the wall and rested against it, while Arley settled down onto Miss Cartwright's chair.

Gun in one hand and one eye on the detective, he began to fumble beneath the desk for the missing key; his movement was steady at first, methodical, but became increasingly frantic as it failed to bear fruit. Finally, he rose, slammed his fist down on top of the desk and kicked out at the chair. He watched it career across the floor and clatter into the far wall.

"Like kicking things, don't you?" said Inky.

Arley seemed not to hear. He thrust his free hand into every conceivable hiding place. The vase of lilies crashed to the floor, and various items of paper scattered like confetti as his search became more desperate. The telephone log book joined the flowers, followed by the telephone itself. One by one, the crazed villain removed each of the draws and slung their contents across the desk. Eaten up with fury, he failed to notice Inky, only feet away, remove the key from his pocket and slip it up his shirt sleeve.

Arley swept his arm across the desktop in a final act of frustration, sending all the items he had piled there tumbling to the floor – an avalanche of pens, paper, paper clips, marbles, rubber bands, plus a calculator and desk calendar. "You said the key was here, Stevens!" he yelled, snatching up his torch and approaching his victim. "Get over there and get me that key!"

Inky headed back to Miss Cartwright's desk, and then began to lower himself to the floor. "I need to kneel to reach it," he said. "It's taped underneath the desktop."

"Oh no, you don't, Stevens. I want to see everything you're doing," said Arley, training both gun and flashlight towards the young detective and partially lighting up the space beneath the desk. "Right, no sudden movements! Get me that key!"

Inky leaned forwards slowly, then disappeared under Ginny

Cartwright's desk.

"I'm warning you, Stevens!" said Arley, straining to see.

Inky pretended to search along the underside of the desk. When he finally reappeared, he raised both hands slowly into the air, ensuring that his captor had a clear view of the key that was now pinched between his thumb and forefinger. Arley's torchlight skimmed across the surface of the small metallic object causing it to glow like copper.

"Good!" said Arley, "Now, I want you to insert it into the lock behind you."

Inky slowly released the door's lock and gently opened it to reveal the Snake's Office, shrouded in blackness.

Without warning, Arley lunged at the young detective, slamming the butt of his shotgun into his ribcage. Inky staggered backwards, doubled over, then dropped to his knees, fighting for air. Arley strode past his crumpled body and into the office, immediately sliding his torch beam over the darkness until it came to rest on the Snake's desk. There, sure enough, was a single A4 piece of paper set in front of her chair. His face lit up with a smile so broad that it lifted his beard, but his triumph was short lived; just as he was weighing up how to dispose of the youth, now surplus to requirements, his fortune changed.

Bang!

In a single movement, Inky summed up what little strength he had to kick shut the office door. It locked in a blink. Almost immediately, shouting erupted from within – the sound of unbridled anger. Vincent Arley, beat against the door with such venom that he injured both his fists. On and on he went, showing no signs of stopping. He yelled. He cursed. He spat, but the door held fast; it was engineered to cope with such an emergency.

Safe at last, Inky surrendered to exhaustion. He leant back against the door and gently slid to the ground. From the floor, he uttered a single word: "Checkmate!"

CHAPTER TWENTY-TWO –
FALLOUT

The sun finally reappeared the following day, peeping out cautiously from behind thick, grey clouds. The resulting daylight emerged thin and reedy, but without any of the menace that the great storm had delivered the day before. It was Ginny Cartwright who discovered the mess littering the Reception, and it was she who discovered the typed note pinned onto the Snake's door. Her mouth fell open as she started to read, and before she'd even reached the end of its second paragraph, she was scrambling to find the telephone.

Miss S.

Please call the police immediately! DO NOT UNLOCK YOUR
OFFICE WITHOUT AN ARMED PRESENCE.

What I'm about to reveal may sound unbelievable, but
when you look at the state of the Reception you'll see that
you need to exercise caution.

We have all been deceived; our caretaker has taken
advantage of the trust Blinkton School has placed in him.
He has previously served a ten-year sentence for armed
robbery, and since arriving here, he has lied and cheated
his way into our confidence. He faked his references and
came to work here to pursue a private vendetta against our
Head of Governors, Lord Marmaduke Merridew, who was the
Crown Court judge who sent him to prison

'Fred Varley' is a false identity. The criminal's real name
is Vincent Arley, and he's inside your office right now,
armed!

On a less urgent note, I feel that it's my duty to inform
you that our Head of Science, Mr Ray Day, lacks any sense
of morality. He is a braggart, a cheat and a bully. Mr
Day's treatment of Mr Whitkirk has been nothing short

of disgraceful, and the complaints our Science Technician brought to your attention yesterday were genuine and deserve re-evaluation. Your decision to dismiss Mr Whitkirk was ill-founded, based as it was on scurrilous lies circulated by Mr Day himself.

Finally, please do not try to identify me. I prefer to remain anonymous, but rest assured that I have the interests of Blinkton High School at heart.

"Miss, you need to come into school as quickly as possible," stuttered Miss Cartwright, when she'd plugged the telephone back in. "This is a real emergency. There's been a lightning strike, and something else has happened. We need to call the Police!"

****

Later that morning, mayhem reigned at the school gate: a fleet of police vans blocked off the end of Wordsworth Drive, and the whole site was cordoned off. Hordes of schoolchildren gathered behind this, four or five deep, chattering excitedly.

The Snake, once she'd arrived, had been desperate to play down the crisis, and dispatched her Deputy to deliver the version of events that had hastily been agreed upon. Mike

Bennett swallowed hard and began: "Last night, our town was hit by the worst storm in its history," he announced to the general throng, "and the school grounds and the school itself have been damaged. The oak tree has toppled and a lightning strike has caused the school's heating system to malfunction. This means we cannot guarantee to keep you safe or warm. Consequently, I regret to inform you that for the next twenty-four hours the school will be closed. There will be no classes."

Silence reigned for precisely one second before chaos exploded, the delight of the students manifesting itself in a cacophony of cheering and arm-waving.

Bennett attempted to maintain order, "But we *will* be open as usual at eight forty-five tomorrow morning—"

The mob booed.

"Listen carefully," shouted Bennett above the clamour, "it's a legal requirement for us to ensure that we provide—" But the rest of his speech was drowned out as the entire school bolted like a flock of startled sheep. Within minutes, the road was empty. All that remained was a lone crisp packet, which spun around wildly, caught up in its own mini-tornado.

****

Two miles away at the town boundary, Wilfred Whitkirk, Blinkton's newly appointed Head of Science, drove his shiny red Peugeot past a rather desperate-sounding road sign:

```
WELCOME TO BLINKTON-ON-SEA
HOME OF THE CODFATHER RESTAURANT.
THANK YOU FOR YOUR VISIT.
(TWINNED WITH MAL-DE-MER, FRANCE)
```

CHAPTER TWENTY-THREE –
HOME SWEET HOME

By the time Inky reached home, the sun was beginning to tinge the horizon purple. A cluster of swallows lined the telegraph wires of Horrobin Lane, contemplating their long journey south.

The detective entered number 13 as silently as possible, and once inside his room, he dropped his coat and rucksack, and buried himself beneath warm bedsheets.

As his breathing finally shallowed, he made a vow to speak to Ross and Rose at the earliest opportunity to pass on his thanks and supply them with as much information as he thought it wise for them to know.

Inky reached under his pillow and felt the reassuring touch of metal: the caretaker's keys. He still had one more mission left to fulfil and having unlimited access to the whole of the school premises would make this easy. Inside his rucksack was the letter he planned to swap for the one inside the brown envelope in his student file at the earliest opportunity:

Mr P Bearon
Chief Resettlement Officer
Sir Thomas Lee Towers
Old Pepper Lane
PO Box 137, Krull

Confidential Memo. re. Master Stevens

To: Miss Trudy Peters, Head of Year Four, Blinkton High School.

Dear Miss Peters,

As you're aware, Master Stevens was relocated to Blinkton High School halfway through his third year under traumatic circumstances. At the same time, he was removed from his mother's care with immediate effect and placed under the care of his mother's sister and brother-in-law, Alice and Eric Garner, pending a review into what would be in the young man's best interests moving forwards.

Now that matters have settled down and a degree of stability restored, it's time to reach a more permanent solution concerning the future of Master Stevens. Mr and Mrs Garner have requested that they be allowed to continue caring for their nephew, and I'm delighted to inform you that the Council has agreed to uphold their request. Henceforward, Master Stevens will be permanently rehoused with them.

Although his previous Head of Year, Mr Brian Passaretto, raised a few concerns about Master Stevens' solitary nature, we are content to overlook these in the light of his good academic progress.

It's long been Council policy to embrace diversity and to champion the uniqueness of every individual. Master Stevens' behaviours, though perhaps more unusual than most, still place him within the range of what is 'normal', and we therefore see no reason to remove him from mainstream schooling.

I am, therefore, pleased to recommend that Master Stevens continues to remain with the Garners and to attend Blinkton High School on a permanent basis. I'd like to thank you for your support in this matter and to advise you that no further action is required.

Yours sincerely,

Paul Bearon- <u>Chief Resettlement Officer.</u>

Inky knew, of course, that he'd have to send a similar letter to Mr Bearon at the Council Offices, courtesy of Miss Trudy Peters, but for the moment, he could relax.

Relieved, Inky allowed his mind to meander towards sleep. Now that the case of the caretaker's keys was over, he could mop up its after effects within a more leisurely timescale. He could move around school at will. At peace, he sighed contentedly.

Then Inky's eyes snapped open, and he sat bolt upright as one dreadful thought flashed across his mind: "Wiggy's still trapped inside the vault!"

***** Case Closed ****